BRAVE HEART

Glad to be leaving London and many unhappy memories, Janine Sherwood moves to Friars Bridge to take up her post as headmistress of the village school. Living in the house owned by school governor Sir Gavin Hampton, Janine and her daughter Tamsyn are comfortably established there. But shadows from the past reach out to haunt her — threatening to shatter the happiness she and Tamsyn have found. Danger surrounds Janine as she fights to save all she holds most dear.

DINEY DELANCEY

BRAVE HEART

Complete and Unabridged

LINFORD
Leicester

First published in Great Britain in 1983 by
Robert Hale Limited
London

First Linford Edition
published 2007
by arrangement with
Robert Hale Limited
London

British Library CIP Data

Delancey, Diney
    Brave heart.—Large print ed.—
Linford romance library
1. Love stories
2. Large type books
I. Title
823.9'14 [F]

ISBN 978–1–84617–604–3

Published by
F. A. Thorpe (Publishing)
Anstey, Leicestershire

Set by Words & Graphics Ltd.
Anstey, Leicestershire
Printed and bound in Great Britain by
T. J. International Ltd., Padstow, Cornwall

This book is printed on acid-free paper

1

There was a strained atmosphere in the staff room where they had been asked to wait. The five people seated there said little, sitting awkwardly waiting for their turn to be interviewed. Several of them had the resigned look of those who are always short-listed and never appointed, and as she gazed round at her rivals for the post, Janine Sherwood felt that her own chances of getting the job were small. She was obviously one of the younger applicants and she was sure that would weigh against her. The others must be more experienced teachers and the job of head, even of a small village school, would not fall to anyone with too little experience.

As she waited Janine reviewed what she had to offer. Her academic qualifications were good and she had experience in several different types of school. In her present job she was deputy head to an elderly headmistress who, although she ran an efficient school and certainly had the welfare of the children at heart, disliked change and had fixed views on education. On many occasions Janine had itched to try out new ideas both in and out of the classroom, but had been thwarted by Miss Hudson's refusal. Was a progressive outlook going to be what this board of managers would be looking for? Janine glanced again at the typed sheet she had been handed by the school secretary when she had first arrived.

'Here are a few notes about the school and a list of our managers,' she had said. 'They like all applicants to know who they're talking to.'

The Reverend Alan Davies headed the list, the vicar. Janine wondered if he would be young or old, enthusiastic or fatigued and waiting to retire. Two women came next, a Mrs Vernon and a Miss Shore, then a Dr Paton, and finally Sir Gavin Hampton Bart., probably the local squire, bluff and hearty, doing his bit on local committees. But this list merely gave the managers' names, it gave Janine no clue as to the sort of person they were looking for.

She gave a start as the door beside her opened and another applicant returned from interview and she felt her heart contract as she heard her own name called. Drawing a deep breath she stood up and, putting an anxious hand to her unruly fair curls and wishing she looked older, went out of the room. Mrs Hope, the retiring head, led her into her office and, having introduced her to the assembled committee, left the room, closing the door behind her.

The vicar was chairman and he smiled at Janine; indicating a chair he said pleasantly, 'Do sit down, Mrs Sherwood.'

Janine did so and looked up to find five pairs of eyes upon her, studying her, assessing her.

'Now then,' the vicar rested his arms

on the desk in front of him and leaned towards her in a confidential manner, 'perhaps you'd like to tell us why you applied for this job.'

Janine began, a little hesitantly at first, and then gaining confidence from their attention, spoke with enthusiasm about her educational experience so far and the ideas and aspirations she had to bring to the job of head of a school.

'Friars Bridge is a small village,' said the woman introduced as Miss Shore, 'how would you see your place in the community in general?'

Janine had been expecting this question and had given some thought to an answer.

'I should want to get to know the families of the children in my care,' she said. 'This is always important, but not always easy in a large city school. In a village I should hope to be more than a teacher, on duty during school hours, I should hope to be approachable enough for any child

4

or its family to come to me should the occasion arise; should they need help.'

'If you were too easily accessible don't you think you might lose the respect and so the authority over your pupils?' The question came from Dr Paton, who had turned out to be a woman. She watched Janine keenly as she waited for her answer.

Janine chose her words carefully.

'If I live in a place it is my home and the other people who live there are my neighbours. That should not alter the way I carry out my responsibilities at school. I have a daughter who will make friends and through her as much as through my work in the school, I hope to become absorbed into the community, contributing what I can and finding my own place within it.'

The managers nodded gravely as they considered her answer. Then the second man, Sir Gavin Hampton, spoke. He was not at all as Janine had pictured him when reading the typed list in the waiting room, not florid and middle-aged, but keen-faced and penetrating.

'Speaking of your daughter, how old is she, by the way?'

'Tamsyn is seven.'

'How would she react to being in a school where her mother was head?'

'She's used to being in a school where I teach, she knows that our relationship is different in the school situation; I don't think the fact that I was the head would alter much for her. She might find it a little harder to be at ease with the other children, but she's an outgoing child and well able to make her own way in the world, independent of me.'

'I believe you are what is termed these days as a 'single-parent family',' said Mrs Vernon. There was the suspicion of a sniff in her voice and Janine looked at her sharply before she answered; indeed, she had difficulty in keeping an edge out of her own voice as she replied, 'I am divorced, yes. My daughter and I are, as you put it, a single-parent family, but we are a family none the less and hold family life very dear.'

'The situation does, however, perhaps present a problem. Supposing your daughter was ill, you would not wish to be away from school for long, yet your daughter would need you. How would you overcome this conflict of duties?'

Janine was on safer ground now, she could appreciate that such a situation must be provided for and she answered evenly, 'I've had to teach throughout Tamsyn's life and on the occasions on which this conflict has occurred so far, my mother, who has no other commitments, has immediately moved in with us and I have never lost more than one day.'

They nodded at her reply and she relaxed again, but her comfort was short-lived as further doubts were cast on her suitability.

'But we have to ask ourselves if someone with personal problems, a broken marriage, behind her, is the person to take responsibility for our children where stability is important, particularly in such a tight-knit community. We could allow no scandal to touch the head of our school. I may seem old-fashioned in this but it is a question which does worry me.' It was Sir Gavin Hampton who spoke, his face unsmiling, nothing in his expression to soften the harshness of his comment. Janine stared at him for a moment and then said, very softly, 'I do not consider that a legitimate question. You are presuming to question my morals; have you similarly insulted the other applicants? I doubt it.'

Sir Gavin seemed quite unperturbed and an awkward silence followed her outburst before she continued, 'It is obviously clear that you should know my situation so that you can judge for yourselves if I am a fit person to take responsibility for your children.' She spoke bitterly, but was determined they should hear her out. 'Harry, my ex-husband, walked out on me when I was expecting Tamsyn. He's never seen her and has made no effort to do so. I'm glad. She's better off without him, as I am. He left and has never returned and he has no legal rights over Tamsyn, the court awarded none. So, we're everything to each other and neither want nor need anything else. There could be no scandal attached to us; Harry won't even know where we are and I am extremely unlikely to contract any other alliance, I have had enough of such relationships. I hope that satisfies you.' She stared defiantly round at them while she thought, 'Well, you've done it now. They'll never give you the job when you've spoken to them like that.'

The Reverend Alan Davies cleared his throat and said awkwardly, 'I'm sorry, Mrs Sherwood, perhaps we should leave your family circumstances and discuss your views on the organisation and running of a school such as ours.'

'Yes,' said Janine abruptly. 'Perhaps

we should.' She was still too angry to notice the dawning respect in their eyes at her reply.

They continued to fire questions at her, obviously relieved to change the turn of the interview; how would she recommend the teaching of poetry to junior children? How did she maintain discipline amongst the older boys? What place had television in the school curriculum? What were her views on the P.T.A.? Should Religious Instruction be a formal subject in the school day? How important were school outings connected with projects developed in school?

Once returned to subjects such as these Janine answered with fluency and conviction; these were topics she had considered and understood and when at last the vicar said, 'Thank you for coming, Mrs Sherwood, it has been most interesting to meet and talk with you,' she stood up feeling she might have redeemed herself a little.

'Oh, there is just one thing more,'

said the vicar. 'If you were offered the job, what would you want to do about a house?'

Janine looked surprised and said, 'I'm sorry, I understood a school house was offered. I should want to accept that offer.'

'Indeed, indeed,' agreed the vicar. 'Only you see, Mrs Hope is still living in the school house and we are loth to evict her just because she has retired, especially after such long service. It has been her home for years.'

'I see.' Janine tried to sound impassive, though it was the offer of a school house as much as anything which had drawn her to apply for this particular job.

'However,' continued the vicar, 'Sir Gavin has very kindly offered Mill Cottage on the Chariswood Estate at the same rent for the new head, so that Mrs Hope can remain undisturbed. It's not next door, of course, as Mrs Hope's house is, but it's within walking distance, just at the edge of the village.'

'I see,' said Janine again, wondering what else she was expected to say.

'Fine, fine,' declared the vicar. 'Ask Mrs Hope for Mr Hollis, please.'

Then came the waiting back in the box of a staff room. Janine found herself studying the repetitions in the wallpaper and wishing she had controlled her outburst, however angry the insinuations of the insufferably arrogant Sir Gavin Hampton had made her.

'How did it go?' Her thoughts were interrupted by another of the applicants, a middle-aged woman with a motherly bosom confined in twin-set and tweeds.

'Difficult to say,' said Janine non-committally, 'they asked so many things and it's hard to tell which answers pleased them and which didn't.'

'Exactly, you can't tell how you're doing!' And the other woman went off into a detailed reconstruction of her own interview. Janine was only half listening to her by the end, but she did notice that apparently no one had asked

the woman about her family background, and felt the usual flame of
anger at the reaction there had been to
her own situation. But she was more
angry at her inability to ignore the
comments and innuendo; goodness
knows she ought to be past that by now,
not always on the defensive.

Others in the waiting room joined in
the general post-mortem while they all
drank tea from an enormous enamel
pot the secretary had brought. The final
applicant was back now and while the
managers deliberated in the office, relief
that it was all over flooded through the
staff room. They had each made their
bid to become head of the village
school in Friars Bridge and now it was
up to the managers to reach their
decision.

They reached it remarkably quickly.
Janine had hardly finished her cup of
tea before Mrs Hope asked her to
return to the office.

'Ah, Mrs Sherwood, please sit down.'
Once again the vicar indicated the

chair. Janine sat down, crossed one well-shaped leg over the other, adjusted her skirt and waited.

'Well, Mrs Sherwood, the board and I agree that if you would accept the post of headmistress of our little school, we should be delighted to offer it to you. We feel we need new, young blood here, someone with an entirely different approach, so that there shall be no comparisons to draw between the old régime and the new. We need someone with drive and enthusiasm, you seem to have both, and we need someone not afraid to face facts and the strength of character to overcome difficulties.' He beamed across the desk at her. 'Will you take it on?'

Janine drew a deep breath and said, 'I'd like to very much, but to do so I must feel I have the confidence of this board; I cannot take on such a job if anyone has reservations about me. I want the job very much, but I will not accept it unless I know your confidence is in me.'

Looking startled, as if when handing out largesse the recipient had enquired if it were honestly come by, the vicar said, 'You are our first choice by a large majority and I have every faith in your ability to do a good job.'

'I was the dissenter,' said Sir Gavin Hampton. 'Since you question the appointment, which is most unusual in such circumstances, I will say to you honestly that I have reservations about your appointment. You were not my first choice. However, I am quite prepared to be convinced, and that of course will be up to you. Are you willing to accept the job on those terms?'

Janine returned his steady gaze and for the first time really took in his strong face, lean and tanned; his deep-set eyes, dark and considering, and his smooth dark hair falling across his forehead.

'I accept,' she said evenly, 'but I shall not consider myself on trial.'

'No, no, of course not,' said the vicar,

'we're happy to leave the school in your hands. Welcome to Friars Bridge, Mrs Sherwood.' He stood up and reached across the desk to shake her hand. So did the other members of the board, Sir Gavin Hampton included, though his handshake was brief and perfunctory.

'You'll be wanting to see the house of course,' he said. 'I'll take you over there if you'd care to wait for a moment.'

'Thank you, Sir Gavin. I should very much like to see it.' And Janine left the meeting to its closing procedures and returned, her heart dancing, to the congratulations of her disappointed rivals. The cloud caused by Sir Gavin's reservations faded into insignificance as she looked forward to moving Tamsyn from their cramped home in the city to a cottage in the village of Friars Bridge; to exchanging her place as a very restricted deputy head for that of head, with freedom to run her own school in her own way. Her heart indeed danced and she was filled with exhilarating anticipation.

When the managers' meeting had broken up, Sir Gavin Hampton came out to her again.

'Have you a car?' he enquired as he searched his pockets for his keys. Janine was glad to be able to say that she had, and so avoid the embarrassment of having to ride in his car with him.

'Then perhaps you'd like to follow me and I'll take you to the house.' She followed his car out of the school yard and drove through the village, over the bridge which spanned the River Flax and gave the village its name and passed the last house in the main street. Then he turned sharp right up a steep hill and there it was, a long narrow house with tiny wooden-framed windows. It stood end-on to the winding lane and faced out across the valley below. The hill rose steeply behind it, sheltering it from the north east wind and protecting its privacy. Sir Gavin swung off the road and pulled into a cleared space before the front wall and Janine eased her car in behind him.

He led the way to the front door set deep in the thick stone walls and opened it with an old-fashioned key.

'It's rather gloomy with no furniture in it,' he said as he stood aside for her to enter, 'but it has great possibilities and you can decorate it how you like, to fit in with your own furniture.'

Janine looked round her. She did not find the house gloomy, though it was dirty and in sore need of redecoration; she saw the shafts of sun piercing the dusty windows and playing on the wooden floor, she saw the wide hearth with blackened stonework promising roaring winter fires, and she knew that this house could be a real home, snug and comfortable.

Sir Gavin left her to wander through the rooms to inspect the rather primitive kitchen and the narrow wooden staircase leading to the rooms above. He made no intrusion while she visualised herself and Tamsyn happily established there. He made no comment as she stared in silence out across the valley and when at last she returned to him, he merely raised his eyebrows in query.

'I should be very happy to make this house my home,' she said simply. 'I know Tamsyn and I can be very comfortable here.'

'Not too big for just the two of you?'

Janine bristled at something in his tone and replied icily, 'So far we have been confined to very small accommodation, we shall enjoy spreading ourselves a little, having a bedroom each.'

He looked at her coolly and said, 'I'm sorry if I upset you, it was unintentional. I didn't want you to feel lonely up here.' But his tone was far from apologetic and Janine quelled her anger with difficulty. She softened her voice as she glanced round her at the bare walls and said, 'This is a lovelier place than any other we have been in.'

Sir Gavin nodded and said, 'That's settled then. Please move in at your convenience.'

'Thank you,' she said. 'It'll probably be early in the summer holidays, to give us plenty of time to get settled before the September term begins.'

'Just come up to Chariswood anytime for the key if you want to measure up for curtains or anything and I'll try and find the spare so that you and your daughter can have a key each when you move in.'

He locked the door behind them and when they reached the cars he turned to shake hands once again.

'I hope you'll be happy here,' he said, still without smiling.

'We shall be,' she replied, 'and never fear, I intend to make a success of this job.'

The moment she was removed from Sir Gavin Hampton's overbearing presence, Janine felt her spirits lift and the excitement bubbling at the news she would have for Tamsyn that evening.

2

The Sherwoods moved to Friars Bridge the first week in August and set to work to make Mill Cottage their own. There was a great deal to do and Tamsyn, full of excitement at the move to a completely different environment, joined in with enthusiasm.

'I'm sorry we shan't have a holiday this summer,' remarked Janine as they paused for elevenses one morning. They had been re-organising the kitchen and there was dust and rubbish in heaps round them. Tamsyn surveyed these and grinned happily at her mother.

'It's all so different,' she replied, 'that it feels like being on holiday all the time. You know, to look out across fields instead of streets and houses. It's better than a holiday to know we'll always be here.'

'It may not be always, darling,'

21

warned Janine, 'but we'll hope it's for some time to come yet. And I know just what you mean. I don't think I'll ever get tired of our view.'

'Can I learn to ride?' asked Tamsyn suddenly. 'It was too expensive in London, but it might not be here.'

Janine smiled, knowing of old her daughter's love of horses. 'We'll see,' she said, 'we've lots of things to find out about, haven't we? Don't worry; we'll add that to our list.'

Gradually they settled in and by the time the school opened for the September term, they had learnt their way around the village, made themselves known at the post office and shop and Janine had spent several days actually in the school, sorting through stock and planning for the coming term. Tamsyn met several children of about her own age playing on the village green and she joined them happily while her mother worked at school, so that when the school opened its doors in early September she had made several friends and was familiar with the school itself.

That first morning filled Janine with a thrill of excitement. She was going to take her first assembly as headmistress, to start her first day in a school of her own. As she faced all the children collected together in the hall, she felt her heart thumping. They were singing a hymn, 'So here has been dawning another blue day', and she watched their faces as they sang, some also facing their first day, wide-eyed and a little afraid; others, the older ones trying to sum her up and wondering what difference it would make to have Mrs Sherwood rather than Mrs Hope, and noticing a gleam in one or two eyes, Janine wondered if these were the ones who would make an early impression on her.

When they had sung their hymn and said a prayer, she sat them all down to talk to them. First she introduced herself and then she said, 'Now I want you to realise that I am not Mrs Hope and I may do things a little differently from the way she did. Don't worry about that, I'll explain what I want you to do and if anyone doesn't understand, just ask. Don't be afraid to come to me with any problems. I want to help. I want to get to know each one of you, and I shall try and get round to talk to every one of you today so that we can begin to know each other at once.'

Thus began an exhuasting day. The children split into their two main groups, infants and juniors, and Mrs Wilder shepherded her infants away to her classroom and Janine's group, the juniors, clattered noisily into their room. It was not difficult to pick out the one or two troublemakers, ready to try her out with sweetly innocent remarks like, 'Mrs Hope didn't do it like that . . . ' 'Please Mrs Sherwood, Mrs Hope always let us . . . '

In fact Janine made very few alterations to the general running of the school. She wanted to get everything going smoothly in its old routine so that she could get the feel of the place; she eased herself in with as little disruption as possible and the changes she had planned were introduced gradually so the smaller innovations went almost unnoticed so easily were they accepted. Mrs Wilder, the infants' teacher, proved easy to work with and because she too was an enthusiastic teacher, they found that they worked well together.

At the end of the first day, just as the children were streaming out into the playground to their waiting mothers, the vicar arrived and was full of questions as to how her day had gone and whether she was comfortably settled in her new home. While Janine greeted him politely and answered his questions easily, inside she felt a flicker, anger or cynical amusement?

'He's come to check up on me,' she thought. 'It'll be Sir Gavin next!' But she scolded herself for the uncharitable thought and tried to see that he had only come to be welcoming and kind. She had not seen Sir Gavin since the day of the interview. When she had called at Chariswood for the keys to Mill Cottage, she was informed by the housekeeper that Sir Gavin and Lady Hampton were away on holiday, but Sir Gavin had left the keys for her to take when she wanted them.

Janine was wrong about him coming to check up on her. He did not even bother to drive over and see if she was comfortably installed in the house on his estate. She did not see him for several weeks into the term. By then the project 'Autumn' was well under way and the school was filled with autumn colours, leaves, fruits and seeds; pictures and stories and poems about preparations made by animals for winter, migrating birds, harvest festival; lengthening shadows and shortening days. Everyone was involved and during those first weeks discreet visits were made by each of the managers, all, that is, except Sir Gavin Hampton. Mrs Hope looked over her garden wall, watching the children working individually round the school ground and in supervised groups on the village green; and then, invited by the children, she came into the school to see the displays of work in the hall and the classrooms. She came to the special school harvest festival in the church as did Mrs Vernon, Miss Shore and Dr Paton; but Sir Gavin Hampton did not appear. Gradually Janine's wariness changed to anger, far from the ever-present overseeing attention she had feared, wondering if he were waiting to pounce if she faltered, it was now apparent that he took no interest in the school at all; he who had declared that she must prove herself, had not even bothered to come and see for himself. But as the days progressed into weeks even this anger died and was forgotten as the school and the children took hold of her, often leaving her exhausted but always with an underlying satisfaction.

She had not finished work on the

house, either, and every spare moment she spent decorating it to suit herself and Tamsyn, and gradually that too developed under her hand so that the cold stone house she had seen on the interview day was quietly transformed into their own home, snug against the coming winter.

One Saturday afternoon in mid-October, Tamsyn said, 'Let's go for a walk, Mum, and then have crumpets for tea.' Janine laid down the work books she had been marking and looked out into the golden afternoon.

'Done,' she said. 'Come on, coats and boots and we'll go up over the hill.'

Minutes later they were striding out along the track leading up the steep hill behind the house. They reached the top and from there could see the country on either side of the ridge. Far below, behind them, was Friars Bridge with the river snaking its way between the houses, then the hills ran in a sharp spine and before them lay a second valley, woodland and pasture in autumnal patchwork and, almost hidden by a clump of trees, was a large house, the smoke from its tall chimneys rising straight and steady into the windless sky.

'That must be Chariswood,' said Janine. 'I've only approached it by the road, but I think that must be it.'

Despite the afternoon sun it was too cold to stand still and together Janine and Tamsyn set off along the ridge away from Chariswood, following a well-defined path, stony in some places and pockmarked with hoof-prints in the muddy patches. It dipped down through a copse and emerged on an open grassy plateau before diving into the trees again, several hundred yards ahead.

'I wish we had a dog,' said Tamsyn suddenly. 'Wouldn't it be lovely to walk him up here? Couldn't we, Mum, couldn't we have a dog? I'd look after him, really. You wouldn't have to do anything, I promise.'

'The problem is the daytime, Tam,'

replied her mother. 'What would we do with him in the day when we're both at school? It wouldn't be fair to leave him alone in the house all day.'

'I could go home at lunchtime and let him out.'

'I don't think that would work,' said Janine. 'There would be days when you couldn't go, choir day for instance.' Choir was another of Janine's innovations and occupied half-an-hour of every Wednesday lunchtime.

'I don't mind missing choir,' said Tamsyn.

'I'm afraid you can't just do that,' said Janine. 'I can't make exceptions for you, you know.'

'It's not fair,' said Tamsyn angrily, 'other children go home for dinner.'

'But their mothers are there with them,' said Janine patiently. 'Your dinner is at school, not at home.'

'It's not fair,' cried Tamsyn again, 'it's horrid you being headmistress, all the others say . . . ' She stopped abruptly and looked across the hillside as she heard the pounding of hooves and a gasp of delight escaped her as a lone rider emerged from the trees, mounted on a beautiful black horse, and cantered easily across the grass towards them. It was Sir Gavin Hampton. He reined in when he saw them and approached them at a walk.

'Good afternoon, Mrs Sherwood.'

'Sir Gavin.'

'This is your daughter, Tamsyn, isn't it?'

Tamsyn beamed at him. 'Yes, I'm Tamsyn. I say, isn't he beautiful.' She reached up to stroke the big horse's muzzle. Janine caught her breath and half-moved to restrain her, but catching her movement Sir Gavin said easily, 'It's all right, Mrs Sherwood, he won't hurt her.' Even so Janine noticed that all the time the little girl was near the horse, Sir Gavin held him collected so that she should be in no danger.

'Isn't it a magnificent afternoon?' he went on. 'I love these late autumn days, sharp and clear. You can see for miles today from up here.'

'Yes, it is beautiful. We haven't been up this way before. Is that your home down over there?' Janine pointed vaguely in the direction of the secluded house they had seen.

'Yes, that's us,' replied Sir Gavin. 'How's it going down at the school?' he asked after a brief pause. 'Settled in now?' Janine felt the familiar flicker of annoyance that he had only now bothered to ask and then only during a chance meeting.

'Yes, thank you,' she said stiffly.

'I hear there's some beautiful art work,' he went on, 'and a collage of autumn leaves right across the end of the hall.' Janine was startled at his knowledge and her surprise must have shown on her face, for he burst out laughing and said, 'You see, what you dreaded all along has happened. I've been checking up on you,' but before she could expostulate he turned his attention to Tamsyn who was still muttering softly to the attentive horse.

'You like horses and ponies, Tamsyn?' he asked.

'Oh yes,' cried the little girl, 'I love them, but I've only done riding at the seaside. Mummy says perhaps I can learn here if it isn't as expensive as in London, but we haven't found out yet. It's on our list for finding out, but we haven't done it yet.' Her words tumbled out in her enthusiasm and at her reference to the cost of riding lessons Janine said 'Tamsyn!' but her daughter continued completely oblivious of her mother's disapproval, 'Do you know where I can ride? Is there a place and is it very expensive, 'cos I've got some birthday money in the post office and perhaps I can give that to Mummy to help with the lessons.'

'Tamsyn!' This time the sharpness of Janine's tone did penetrate and Tamsyn swung round to look enquiringly at her mother and seeing her expression said, 'What? What's the matter?' Unwilling to get into any prolonged explanations or arguments, Janine said, 'I'm sure Sir

Gavin is anxious to get on, and he won't want his horse to get cold.'

Immediately Tamsyn jumped aside exclaiming, 'No, of course he mustn't get cold.' But Sir Gavin did not move on immediately. 'My nieces have a pony that's so fat it's called Barrel. They keep him at Chariswood because they live in London. They come down occasionally to ride him, but he spends most of his time in the paddock. I wonder if you'd like to come over and ride him, Tamsyn?' Tamsyn was ecstatic. 'Oh yes, please,' she breathed, her eyes brilliant with happiness; but Janine was horrified.

'She couldn't, I mean she can't ride. I mean, well, it's your nieces' pony, what will they say?' She stammered to a halt, not knowing what else to say, loth to be under any obligation whatsoever to Sir Gavin Hampton, yet catching sight of her daughter's ecstatic face, longing to give her her heart's desire. Sir Gavin saw Tamsyn's face and then Janine's and knew the thoughts of both.

'Come on,' he said gently, 'let her come over and ride him. I've a stable lad who'll teach her to ride properly and she'll come to no harm.'

Janine was still torn. 'We couldn't impose on you like that.'

'It wouldn't be an imposition — in many ways it would do me a favour. The pony needs exercise and he's too small for us to ride. If Tamsyn would like to come we'd be pleased to see her, and once she's been introduced to Ned, the lad, she can come over whenever it suits them both; but of course it's up to you.'

The black horse was growing restless, pawing the ground, and it was clear he was eager to be away. Tamsyn turned beseeching eyes on her mother.

'Please, Mummy! Please say I can go.'

'Bring her tomorrow afternoon and she can have a go and see how she gets on.' Sir Gavin got ready to move off as he spoke and Janine found herself saying, 'Well, if you're sure. Thank you very much. It's really very kind of you.'

'See you tomorrow, Tamsyn,' said Sir Gavin. 'I'll tell Barrel you're coming. Good afternoon, Mrs Sherwood.' And he trotted on towards his home.

Tamsyn threw her arms about Janine's neck, almost knocking her over in her excitement.

'Mummy, isn't it just marvellous? Mummy, isn't it?' And knowing she would never hear the last of it if they did not take Sir Gavin up on his offer, Janine sighed and hugging her excited daughter back, said, 'Yes, marvellous. Come on, let's work up an appetite for those crumpets.'

3

After lunch the following day, Janine and Tamsyn drove to Chariswood. Tamsyn wore jeans, polo-neck sweater and wellington boots in anticipation of her ride, while her mother was dressed in close-fitting slacks and silky shirt, topped with an open-weave poncho. Before dressing, Janine had given no little thought as to what to wear, though she did not want to visit Chariswood in her casual weekend clothes, neither did she want to dress up like a town-dweller on a country weekend, and she hoped that what she eventually chose would split the difference; at least the clothes were all favourites and their easy familiarity gave her a certain measure of confidence.

They drove up the drive and parked outside the house. Chariswood was a large grey stone house; the original part, probably a substantial farmhouse, had been added to and extended at different times; its austere lines had been embellished by one of its Georgian owners and a Victorian had built on a wing facing south to catch the sun. The grey slate roof was topped by huge decorated chimneys and from one of these blue-grey smoke twisted gently into the air, undisturbed by wind on this quiet October Sunday. The windows and doors were closed against the autumnal chill and the house seemed silent and withdrawn.

For a moment Janine was at a loss, whether to march up to the imposing front door or to go in search of a less conspicuous entrance. Tamsyn, however, had no such inhibitions; bursting with excitement she leapt from the car and strode up to the front door to tug at the old iron bell-pull. Hurriedly Janine got out of the car to follow her, but before she reached the front door there was a crunch of gravel and Sir Gavin appeared round the house, accompanied by two black labrador dogs who rushed forward to investigate the newcomers. Tamsyn's face split into a grin at the sight of them and she cried, 'Oh, what lovely dogs, what're their names?'

'Jason and Samson,' replied Sir Gavin. 'Hallo, Mrs Sherwood, I'm glad you came.'

At that moment the front door opened in reply to Tamsyn's summons on the bell. Sir Gavin spoke to the housekeeper who had answered.

'Ah, Mrs Deeben, would you mind telling Lady Hampton there'll be two extra for tea.' He turned to Tamsyn. 'I'm sure you'll feel like something to eat when you've had your ride, won't you?' And before Janine could protest, Tamsyn replied with enthusiasm, 'Yes, please.'

Sir Gavin smiled at both of them and said, 'Let's go and find Ned. He's been saddling up Barrel for you, Tamsyn.'

Feeling he had trapped her into a position of disadvantage by addressing his remarks to Tamsyn, Janine followed behind, watching her daughter skipping along happily beside Sir Gavin, for all the world like a third labrador, an immediate rapport established between them. She knew she was stupid to feel annoyed, Tamsyn could not have been happier and it was Sir Gavin Hampton who was supplying this happiness and yet Janine was angry and the very stupidity of the emotion made it worse.

Sir Gavin led the way to the stable yard where a cheerful lad of about eighteen was saddling a small grey pony. Tamsyn let out a cry of delight and rushed to the pony and flung her arms about his neck. The pony, apparently entirely unmoved by this, blew down his nostrils and waited for her to mount. Janine kept well in the background and watched with interest as Tamsyn was shown the proper way to mount, how to sit and hold the reins; on instruction the child stuck her short legs out, as Ned adjusted the stirrups to the right length, and then prepared to ride.

'Just a minute,' said Sir Gavin, 'you need a hard hat. Ned, see if Annabel's hat is in the tack room.'

Ned vanished into one of the stable buildings and returned at once with a proper riding hat which he put on Tamsyn's head.

'Right,' said Sir Gavin satisfied, 'off you go. Take it steady, Ned.' Ned began leading the fat little pony and his rider across the cobbled yard, towards the gate of the adjacent paddock. Sir Gavin, about to follow, turned at last to Janine.

'Aren't you coming to watch?'

'Yes, of course,' she replied and crossed the yard behind them.

The lesson was a tremendous success; Tamsyn perched on Barrel, listening with marked attention to the instructions Ned gave her, and beamed with delight as first they walked and then they trotted round the paddock.

A pale October sun smiled on them, burnishing the last brave beech leaves clinging to the trees in the copse beside the house. Janine caught the scent of a bonfire smouldering and sniffed appreciatively, loving the earthy smells of autumn and the crispness in the air.

'My favourite sort of day, too' said Sir Gavin, as if she had spoken her thought and Janine turned, surprised to find him watching her rather than the riding lesson. The dogs sprawled at his feet and he was leaning easily on the paddock fence, one foot resting on the bottom rail as he studied her and smiled at what he saw. Angry at his cool appraisal Janine did not reply, but turning back to the paddock gave her attention to her daughter and Ned. Completely unabashed by her silence, Sir Gavin did not attempt to break it or move away, he continued to lean comfortably on the fence enjoying the afternoon air. Tamsyn was learning to rise to the trot now, and though Janine was apparently watching her she was suddenly very aware of the man beside her, not as a remote figure with whom she had a nodding acquaintance, but as a man. Without turning her head she could see his hands clasped lightly together as his arms rested on the wooden rail of the fence; they were tanned with long fingers and there was a subtle strength in them which made her catch her breath. She longed to look again at his face, to study him as he had her, but she did not want to show that his presence had made any impression on her. It was a long time since she had felt the force of a man's personality emanating from him so strongly that it was almost tangible, that she had been affected by a man's masculinity. Since Harry left she had closed her mind and her heart to relationships of any depth and the overtures she had received from men she had met, had been so strongly repulsed that they had never been renewed. She felt unsteady and unsettled in the presence of Sir Gavin Hampton and she did not like it; particularly when she remembered Lady Hampton was in the house waiting for them to join her for tea.

The silence between them remained unbroken until Ned finally led Barrel over to them with Tamsyn still perched triumphantly on his back.

'Well done,' said Janine as Tamsyn dismounted and gave Barrel the sugar she had brought specially in her jeans pocket. 'Did you enjoy it?'

'Oh Mummy, it was super. Can I come again and learn some more?' Before Janine could answer Sir Gavin said, 'You can indeed, if your mother agrees; but you haven't finished today yet. Go with Ned and he'll show you how to deal with the saddle and bridle, and you can put Barrel into his stable.'

'Oh thank you,' breathed Tamsyn, her eyes shining.

'Bring her round to the kitchen door when you've finished, Ned, and she can leave her boots there before she comes in for tea.'

Determined that they should leave as quickly as possible, Janine said, 'We can't stay for tea as well. It really is very kind of you, but you've given up enough of your Sunday already.'

'It's entirely up to you of course,' replied Sir Gavin, 'but I'm sure there's a pot made by now and we'd love you both to come in if you can spare the time.'

Unwilling to appear rude after the Hamptons had given Tamsyn her heart's delight, Janine said, 'Well, thank you, just a quick cup then.'

Sir Gavin led the way into the house through a conservatory. He paused at the inner door to remove his own boots and put on his shoes and then took Janine through into the drawing room where Lady Hampton waited, dozing over her book in a deep armchair by the fire. She jerked awake as Sir Gavin strode in. Crossing to the wide fireplace he bent to kiss her cheek.

'Here we are, mother. Let me introduce Mrs Sherwood, I don't think you've met her before. Is tea coming in? It's colder than you think outside and we could do with a cup.'

'It'll be in in a moment,' she replied and turning to Janine who had hesitated in the doorway she said, 'Do come to the fire, Mrs Sherwood, you must be cold if you've been standing about in the paddock. Once the sun goes there's very little warmth in the air.' She smiled and indicated another armchair across the fireplace from her own. 'Come and get warm.'

'Thank you, Lady Hampton.' Janine's voice was a little husky and she cleared her throat nervously as she sat down by the fire.

'How did Tamsyn's lesson go? Did she get on all right?'

'She did very well,' said Sir Gavin. 'She has a natural seat and gentle hands; not something easy to teach.'

'She loved it,' said Janine, wondering at Lady Hampton knowing Tamsyn's name, 'and Sir Gavin has kindly said she can come again, but you mustn't let her become a nuisance. She mustn't interfere with Ned's other work.'

Lady Hampton smiled. 'My dear, don't worry about that, if she's as horse-minded as it seems she'll probably be as happy as anything to help him with mucking out and cleaning tack. As far as we're concerned she may come whenever she likes, mayn't she, Gavin?'

'She may,' he agreed. 'If she'd like to come over after school I'm sure Ned could give her a ride each day.'

Janine looked doubtful. 'I don't know. It'll be getting dark earlier and earlier, by the time I've finished at school . . .'

'It's up to you entirely,' said Lady Hampton. 'You make whatever arrangements you like with Ned. Perhaps she could walk up over the hill by herself. There's a footpath from the top down here and you could fetch her when you're ready. You do exactly what you like, we're just pleased to get the pony exercised.'

Tamsyn arrived soon after the tea trolley and tucked into the sandwiches, cake and biscuits which had been provided for her. When she came in Janine said to her, 'This is Lady Hampton, Tamsyn, say how do you do.'

'How do you do, Lady Hampton?' Tamsyn said solemnly and then added with childish innocence, 'Are you Sir Gavin's wife? You look too old.'

Janine, horrified, nearly choked on her tea, but Lady Hampton with a twinkle in her eye, answered the question seriously, saying, 'No, I'm not his wife, he hasn't got one, I'm his mother. That's why I look old.'

'I see, like my Granny.'

'Yes, I'm a Granny too. Annabel and Caroline, who own Barrel, are my grandchildren.'

When Janine could tear Tamsyn away from the tea table, she stood up to go and thanked Sir Gavin and Lady Hampton.

'It's been lovely to meet you,' said Lady Hampton. 'I'll tell you what, has Tamsyn any jodhpurs? I think there's an old pair of Annabel's upstairs which might fit her.'

'That's very kind of you,' began Janine, 'but I'll get her some of her own if she keeps up her interest and enthusiasm.'

'Of course,' agreed Lady Hampton. 'In the meantime perhaps she'd like to borrow these, they might be more comfortable.'

'Please Mummy, can I?' cried Tamsyn. 'It'd be brilliant to have my own jods.'

Lady Hampton waited for Janine reluctantly to agree before she said, 'You come with me, Tamsyn, and we'll see if we can find them.' The old lady and the child hurried from the room and Sir Gavin said, 'Mother's pleased to give them to her you know, you mustn't take offence.' Janine had indeed felt a flash of anger at the offer of the jodhpurs, even though she knew it was a stupid reaction and that she would have accepted them readily enough from anyone else, but at the back of her mind was an almost unconscious need to prove to the overbearing Sir Gavin that she was well able to provide for her own child, even though he had never suggested that she could not. She was annoyed too that he had noticed her momentary reaction, but she bit back the retort which had risen to her lips and forced herself to say, 'It's very kind of Lady Hampton, Tamsyn'll be over the moon if they fit.'

'Shall I warn Ned to expect her after school? It's up to you.'

Janine wished the Hamptons would not keep assuring her that each decision was 'up to her', whilst placing her in such a position that it was almost impossible to refuse. It was all kindly intended of course, but having had to strive for herself for so long, Janine had an inbuilt aversion to obligations and favours, and the Hamptons' open-handed kindness coupled with her own pride made her feel awkward; however, knowing what it would mean to Tamsyn, she said, 'Thank you. Tam'll be delighted. I'll pick her up afterwards.' Janine spoke calmly, but inside she was troubled; apart from her independent pride, she was not at all sure she wanted to come to Chariswood every day, bringing herself into closer contact with Sir Gavin. She found him disturbing and now she had discovered there was no Lady Hampton, wife and mother, standing between them, she felt even less comfortable than before.

Tamsyn and Lady Hampton returned carrying the old jodhpurs and they all went out into the chilly darkness to the car.

'Thank you again,' Janine said, 'Tamsyn's thrilled.'

'I'll see you at the managers' meeting a week on Wednesday,' said Sir Gavin.

Janine, who had completely forgotten the meeting scheduled for that Wednesday afternoon, said, 'Oh yes, of course. I'll see you then.' And in a chorus of goodbyes and thanks from Tamsyn, they drove away, leaving Sir Gavin and his mother to return to their fireside and discuss the day.

4

From that Sunday Tamsyn never missed a day's riding at Chariswood. The moment school was over she would call a hurried goodbye to her mother and rush home to change into the borrowed jodhpurs, then she raced up the track to the hilltop where they had first met Sir Gavin on horseback and scampered down the steep footpath to Chariswood sheltering snugly among its trees. She spent a blissful hour riding Barrel before grooming him, and watering the other horses and generally helping Ned around the stables. By the time Janine drove round to fetch her it was almost dark and Tamsyn would fall into the car exhausted and smelling of pony, ready for supper, bath and bed. Gone were the days when she hung about the village green waiting for her mother to finish at school or went home to flop listlessly in front of the television until Janine returned. She was delighted with her new life and once Janine was convinced that the Hamptons really had no objections to her perpetual attendance in the stables, she too was pleased to see Tamsyn so happily employed. Never during the first week did she meet Sir Gavin when she went to collect Tamsyn in the evenings, and only once did her path cross Lady Hampton's. That lady greeted her with pleasure.

'My dear Mrs Sherwood. Ned tells me Tamsyn is coming on beautifully and is very keen to help him.'

Janine smiled. 'I'm so glad. You don't know what a boost it's given her. Her talk is all of horses and she assures me she's going to run her own riding stables when she leaves school.'

Lady Hampton laughed. 'They all go through that,' she said. 'My daughter did and Annabel and Caroline are just the same. They'll be here sometime during the Christmas holidays I expect.

Tamsyn'll get on with them like a house on fire.'

'Just as long as she isn't getting in your way or outstaying her welcome.'

'My dear, I never see her and Gavin's away until early next week; but she won't worry him when he is back. It's a full-time job running this estate. We don't have a manager, Gavin does it all himself.' Tamsyn joined them at that moment and nothing further was said about Sir Gavin, for which Janine was grateful. Even the mention of him disturbed her and she was pleased to escape Chariswood knowing she did not have to face him again until the managers' meeting the following week, when she would be on her own ground.

On the morning of that Wednesday, Janine caught herself surveying her reflection more critically in the mirror than normal and, pulling herself up sharply, she thought, 'Janine! What are you doing? You're like a kid of seventeen again!' Then she smiled ruefully and said, 'Well you're hardly

54

likely to make any vast impression on a baronet, not your social scene, but it's nice to know you're interested. Welcome back to the land of the living.'

The meeting was held in the school during the afternoon and though it was not over before the children went home, Janine had no worries about Tamsyn. She knew she would be off over to Chariswood in the usual way. She gave her full attention to the meeting in hand. The vicar was in the chair and in his opening remarks he congratulated Janine on her smooth takeover of the school.

'It really has been a pleasure to see the way the children have taken to you, Janine. I know the other managers have been as interested in your work as I have.'

'You've certainly been in enough,' thought Janine, 'all keeping an eye on me.' But these thoughts remained unsaid and she simply murmured her thanks. When at last the business was concluded and the meeting broke up,

Sir Gavin spoke to her. He had remained silent during much of the meeting, listening intently, but contributing little to the discussions, other than endorsing Janine's intention to try and arrange a school journey to a field centre the following summer.

'I haven't had a chance to see the displays you have set up in the hall yet. Would you mind if I look round?'

Rather surprised Janine replied, 'Help yourself — there's more in the classrooms of course.'

He wandered off, and Janine put her papers together and got ready to go home. The hour had changed at the weekend and though it was not yet getting dark there was a deepening greyness in the sky and the lights were on in the school buildings. She went round to switch them off and found Sir Gavin still in her classroom looking at the leaf prints the children had made and mounted on the wall.

'Are you waiting to go?' he asked. 'I won't keep you.'

'I'm in no hurry, but I don't want to be too late fetching Tam.'

'She's really going to be a good horsewoman if she keeps up the way she's going. Next thing you know you'll be doing the gymkhana circuit in the summer.'

Janine laughed and said, 'We'll sort that out when the summer comes. She'll probably have gone off the boil completely by then; anyway, I expect your nieces'll be anxious to have their pony back to ride themselves in the summer.'

They let themselves out of the school and as they reached their cars Sir Gavin said, 'I have to fetch my mother now, she's got a meeting in the village. I'll bring Tamsyn home if you like.'

'Oh no, it's quite all right, I couldn't let you,' replied Janine hastily. 'I can fetch her as usual.'

'Well, that's silly,' said Sir Gavin. 'I've got to come back here in the next hour anyway, it'll be no trouble to drop her off. Save your time and petrol. I can see you've taken work with you. It'll give you a chance to get some done in peace.'

Feeling it would be ungracious to refuse yet again, Janine thanked him and drove home. After a quick cup of tea she settled to her marking and was more than half-way through it before there was a knock at the front door. As she laid aside her work and went to answer it Janine heard a car coming up the hill, and when she opened the door she saw Sir Gavin stopping outside the gate and was aware of a scuffling in the dark garden as if someone was pushing his way through the bushes and over the wall on to the hill. She flicked on the outside light, but could see nothing of the person who had knocked and run away.

'Mummy,' called Tamsyn from the gate, 'Sir Gavin's brought me home so I've asked him in for a drink.' She spoke in such an innocently adult way that there was little Janine could do about it. The invitation had obviously been accepted, as Sir Gavin followed Tamsyn up the path, so with an inward sigh Janine said, 'If you're entertaining, my girl, you'd better go and change out of those clothes. You pong of Barrel!'

'All right, I won't be a minute.' Tamsyn disappeared up the stairs and Janine stood aside to let her unexpected visitor into the house.

'I hope you don't mind,' said he, 'but she was most insistent.'

'She can be,' agreed Janine. 'But I'm afraid I haven't much to offer you, only sherry.'

'Sherry would be fine, if you're sure.' He looked round the living room, cosy in the lamplight. A fire glowed in the wide fireplace, and warm red curtains Janine had made, caught the glow and increased the warmth. There was not much furniture, but the chairs looked comfortable and old and the table and sideboard reflected the firelight in their lovingly polished surface. A tall grandfather clock ticked rhythmically in a corner, bringing the room to life with its steady beat.

'You've done a good job in here,' remarked Sir Gavin. 'What a transformation!'

'You did say I could do what I liked,' said Janine a little defensively, wondering if Sir Gavin had accepted Tamsyn's invitation to give him a chance to see exactly what she had done. After all, he owned the cottage so she supposed she could not blame him, but as if guessing her thoughts Sir Gavin said, 'I've not come to check up on you, you know; Tamsyn was so keen for me to come in, she said that as you'd been to tea at our house I must come in to yours.'

Janine laughed a little self-consciously and said, 'Please don't worry, I'm pleased to see you.' An awkward silence fell for a moment and to break this as much as anything Janine said, 'Someone knocked on the door as you came up the hill, but by the time I got there he'd run off. I heard whoever it was scuffling in the bushes, but I couldn't see anyone.'

* * *

'I didn't see anyone,' said Sir Gavin, 'perhaps it was one of your kids. Very daring to bang on the headmistress's door and run away!'

'Oh, almost certainly it was. I can guess who, too. I don't mind once, but I hope it doesn't become a habit.'

Janine poured them each sherry and as she handed Sir Gavin his, Tamsyn reappeared dressed in a skirt and jersey.

'That's better, Tam,' said her mother. 'There's a coke in the kitchen if you want one.'

'Yes please,' said Tamsyn and was soon back with her drink to join the adults in the living room.

'Do you know, Mum,' she remarked conversationally as she settled herself on the hearthrug, 'that man was there again today, he asked me where I lived.'

'What man?' Janine spoke sharply and Tamsyn looked up at her in surprise.

'Didn't I tell you yesterday? There

61

was a man sitting on the top of the hill. I think he's a bird-watcher 'cos he had some binoculars round his neck.'

'What was he doing?' asked Janine as calmly as she could.

'Just sitting. He asked me my name and where I was going yesterday.'

'Did you tell him?'

'Yes, why not?'

'I've told you so often, darling, you are not to talk to strangers, particularly when you're alone,' she lowered her voice a little and added urgently, 'particularly when you're up on the hill.'

'I only told him that and then I went on. I didn't want to be late at Chariswood.'

'And he was there again today?' Sir Gavin asked this time.

'Yes,' Tamsyn turned to him, 'today he asked where I lived and I said Mill Cottage, but that I was in a hurry. I didn't stop.'

'Tam, if you want to watch 'Dr. Who', you'd better go and have your bath. I don't mind you staying up as long as you're in your pyjamas, ready for bed.' Janine changed the subject deftly and Tamsyn, eager to watch her programme, went off to her bath without complaint.

'Do you think I should call the police?' Janine asked Sir Gavin as soon as the child was out of hearing.

'Not yet,' he replied. 'You bring her over in the car tomorrow and I'll go up there at about the time she usually comes and find out who this man is and what he thinks he's doing. Time enough for the police after that if necessary. Don't worry, we'll get them here fast enough if his explanations aren't satisfactory, and in the meantime Tamsyn's in no danger if she doesn't go that way.'

Janine agreed to his suggestion, but as she showed him out a few minutes later she wondered if she should go ahead and warn the police anyway. She considered it as she returned to her fireside, but decided against; the police would want a description which would mean them talking to Tamsyn and though she wanted her daughter to be careful, she did not want to make so much of the incident that the child was afraid to venture out alone.

5

The second knock at the door came sometime after Janine had tucked Tamsyn up in bed. She was sitting by the fire, the remains of her supper on a tray beside her, correcting the last in her pile of books. The knock was so soft that at first she thought she had imagined it. She listened, but all she could hear was the sound of the wind, driving the rain in staccato bursts against the window. Then it came again, a little louder, more insistent and Janine went quietly to the front door. She was expecting no one and feeling suddenly alone and vulnerable, she put up the chain before she eased the front door open.

'Jani? It's me, can I come in?' Janine paled at the sound of his voice, whispered and urgent. 'Please let me in quickly.'

With shaking hands she slid the chain free and opened the door wide enough to admit him. He scuttled inside and pushed the door shut behind him, shooting the bolts and replacing the chain, while Janine stared at him helplessly. He stood for a moment, rain streaming off his dirty raincoat to collect in pools round his feet on the floor. He was unkempt, sagging against the hallstand like a rag doll with no stuffing. For a moment she glimpsed defeat in his eyes, then he seemed to draw himself together physically and mentally.

'Is the back door locked?' he enquired anxiously. Janine glanced at the kitchen and said, 'Yes, I think so.' But he had to be certain and pushed past her to check.

Finally satisfied, he came into the living room where Janine was waiting, pale-faced and indignant. He had removed his soaking raincoat, tossing it over the hallstand and now he paused in the doorway and they regarded each other in silence for a moment before he said, 'It's good to see you, Jani, you haven't changed.'

'Well, it's not good to see you, Harry, you have changed,' she answered icily, 'and I don't want to see you any more so perhaps you'd leave before I call the police.' She made a move towards the telephone, but he almost shouted at her, 'No, no — don't. I'll explain. Just let me explain why I've come.'

Seeing his nervousness Janine relaxed a little and said, 'You can have five minutes, not a second more.'

Harry came over to the fire and crouched in front of it, warming his hands; they were blue with cold and it was then that Janine noticed how scruffy Harry was looking, how pinched and cold his face. He did not speak and she said, 'Five minutes isn't very long, Harry, don't waste it if what you have to say is important.' He turned to her then, a little colour creeping back into his pale cheeks and said, 'I'm on the run. I've nowhere to go. I need help.'

'Well, you've come to the wrong place,' said Janine quietly. 'I wouldn't help you if we were the last two people on earth.'

'Come on Jani,' his tone was rallying, 'don't be like that. We had some good times.'

'For God's sake, Harry!' she exclaimed. 'Good times! Did you think of that when you walked out on me and left me seven months pregnant, penniless with the bailiffs at the door?' She stared at him, the years of bitterness welling up inside her, and saw again in his face the weakness which had caused him to leave in the first place; the same fear lurking behind his pale eyes and she found herself despising him for his superficiality, his excuses and his failure to face up to life.

'She's a lovely girl,' he said. 'Tamsyn, Mum told me you'd called her. Pretty name for a pretty girl.'

Sudden light dawned and Janine said, 'It was you! You were the man on the hill, the man with the binoculars asking her questions. It was you.'

He nodded and said, 'You shouldn't let her go about on her own like that, anyone could be up there, molest her or something.'

Now Janine was really angry. 'How dare you,' she whispered, her voice cold with fury, 'how dare you tell me how to bring up my daughter.' She laid stress on the word 'my'.

'She's my daughter too.'

'She is not. You waived all claim to her when you walked out and now after nearly eight years you try and wander back into our lives as if nothing had happened. Well you can't. We don't need you, we don't want you. Get out of here and never come back.'

'Jani, listen . . . '

'Don't call me that awful name.'

'Janine. Please, I'm in trouble.'

'You always were,' said Janine unsympathetically. 'I suppose you want to borrow money.'

'No, at least I wouldn't say no to a few pounds, but that's not it.' His eyes kept returning to the tray beside Janine's chair. 'I could eat some of that bread and cheese,' he said. With a sigh Janine pushed the tray over to him.

'When did you last eat?' she asked and when he told her not for nearly forty-eight hours she relented a little and retired to the kitchen to cook him a plate of sausage, bacon and eggs, butter some bread and make coffee. He did not follow her into the kitchen, but flopped into a chair in front of the fire to wait. When at last she carried the replenished tray back into the living room he was asleep. She shook him and he awoke with a start, leaping from the chair and nearly knocking the supper tray to the floor.

'Sorry,' he mumbled as he sank back into the chair, 'dozed off. You made me jump.' It took him very few minutes to empty the plate Janine set before him, then he leant back nursing the mug of coffee.

'Now,' said Janine firmly, 'you'd better tell me what all this is about

— before you leave.' Her anger had drained away and as she watched him wolfing down the supper she had made him, she found herself quite uninterested. She felt absolutely nothing for him, her love had been extinguished years ago, trampled to death by his callous departure and drowned in the silence that followed. She had neither seen nor heard from him since the day he went; she had divorced him in his absence and nursed her hatred of him. Now as she saw him sitting there before her, thinner and smaller than she had remembered, unshaven, with enormous staring eyes, still afraid of she knew not what, she realised that there was nothing in this husk of a man for her to hate and she could regard him with no feeling at all, as if he were a complete stranger.

'Where have you been since you left?' She had no interest any more, but he seemed to need to talk and perhaps she owed him that before she pushed him out into the night.

'Prison.'

It was such an unexpected reply that Janine stared at him.

'Prison?' she repeated. 'What on earth for?'

'Dope peddling.'

'What! Harry, how could you? Drugs!'

'It was a matter of necessity my dear,' his superficial charm slipped like a mask across his face so that he smiled at her in the way he always had, apparently unperturbed by what he had done. But now, no longer a victim of that charm, Janine was unimpressed by it, and listened with growing distaste to what he told her.

'We were up to our ears in debt and some of the creditors were growing mighty pressing.'

'We! We were in debt! You, you mean.'

'It's the same thing in the end. I took a very well-paid second job and for a while I paid off the worst debts, but I never got really clear.'

'You were gambling.' Janine was no longer accusing as she would have been if she had discovered the fact eight years ago, just wearily making a statement.

'They were debts of honour,' Harry conceded.

'Honour!' scoffed Janine, 'you don't know the meaning of the word.' Harry ignored her comment and said, 'I'd been part of a chain for some time — not a big link at first, but gradually I got to be important enough to know a few people and to be known. There's no escape from that sort of set-up once you're in, but then, when I left you, I had to get out and fast. Some of our lot had been picked up by the police and were likely to blow the whistle on the rest of us. I left the country and stayed away until I thought I was safe.' He grimaced. 'Got picked up on my way back.'

'And you've been in prison ever since?'

'I still should be. I was allowed out to

visit my mother, she's in hospital; she's dying.'

'I'm sorry,' said Janine sincerely. 'I did keep in touch for a while, but she wasn't very encouraging and I let it all drop. She met my mother occasionally but made no effort to visit me or Tamsyn.'

'She knew where you were though, that's how I found you. I had to get out of that place. I'm a marked man and sooner or later they'd have got me.' The smooth veneer of his expression cracked across and his face was grey with fear. He looked nervously at the window to be sure the curtains were closely drawn.

'What do you mean?' asked Janine, used to his overdramatising, but recognising he was truly afraid this time.

'They think it was me who grassed in the first place, that I informed to escape the organisation, and so escaped the police net as well.'

'And did you?' asked Janine and knew she should not have. Harry's eyes shifted uneasily from her face and without answering her question he went on.

'They think that's why I got a light sentence. Five years. They call that a light sentence. It's a lifetime in there. And now someone's put the finger on me and they're trying to get rid of me. There've been a couple of near-accidents already. They're out to get me. They think I'm dangerous, that I know more than I've said and that I mean to use my knowledge. I could if I wanted to, but it's my insurance, they'll be worse off if they kill me, it'll all come out if they kill me.' His voice rose almost hysterically and then he laughed raucously, a chilling sound.

His fear was contagious and Janine felt herself being infected by it.

'What did you come here for? Why did you come here?'

Harry looked at her helplessly. 'I'd nowhere else to go.'

'You really think someone is out to kill you?'

'Yes, I'm sure.'

'And you've led the killers here to me, to Tamsyn?'

'They don't know where I am.' He spoke half-heartedly, abashed by the cold fury of her question.

She answered him softly. 'If you can find me, so can they. So will the police.'

'Please Jani.' He corrected himself. 'Janine. I only need a few days to stay hidden, while I make some arrangements. Like I said, I've got some insurance and when I've organised that then I'll get right away, never trouble you again. I promise I'd never be seen outside the house.'

'No.' Janine's answer was unequivocal.

'Christ, Janine! You're not going to turn me out? Is that all I mean to you?'

'Harry, you mean nothing to me. Not now. Once I'd have done anything for you; now, well I won't tell the police you've been here. That's all. I should do, particularly as I think by the sound of it you'd be safer with them than loose on the world. But you are not staying here — not even for tonight — I don't want Tamsyn to see you.'

'She's already seen me,' pointed out Harry, in a last attempt to sway her. 'Supposing I tell her who I am?'

'If you so much as bat an eyelid in her direction, I'll be on to the police so fast your feet won't touch the ground from here to the police station.'

He looked at her and recognised her determination. Resigned, he shrugged. 'Can I have another cup of coffee before I go?'

'I'll make you one and then you're out of the door and of our lives, and don't dare come back. We don't need you or want you.'

'Don't worry, I get the message. I saw you were well set up with someone earlier. Worth a bob or two by the look of him. Nice motor.'

For a moment Janine was startled and then she gave a short laugh.

'Don't be ridiculous, Harry, he's one of the school managers, almost my employer. He was dropping Tamsyn home, that's all. I suppose it was you scuffling in the bushes when I came to the door.'

'Just being discreet, didn't want to ruin your chances,' smirked Harry.

'Running scared more likely,' muttered Janine, and then added 'I'll get your coffee, then out.'

'Thank you, darling.' Harry was elaborately grateful and she went into the kitchen. While she waited for the water to boil she could hear Harry moving around and wondered what he could be doing, but anxious not to get involved in further conversation, she did not go back and see. When she rejoined him in the living room he had collected his damp raincoat from the hall and was dressed ready to leave.

He drank his coffee quickly and she said, 'Now, go.'

'I suppose you haven't got any money, Jani?'

'I've about ten pounds,' said Janine wearily.

'That'd do,' said Harry and clutching the handful of pound notes she gave him, he stuffed them into his pocket and then reached over and kissed her forehead. 'See you, kid,' he said, and switching off the hall light and the outside light before he eased the front door open, he slid out into the wind and rain.

Janine shut the door swiftly behind him and had it bolted and chained in an instant. Suddenly she felt very weak and she staggered back into the living room and collapsed into her chair, shaking. She found herself staring blankly up at the mantlepiece and it was several moments before her gaze registered that something was missing. It was her picture of Tamsyn, one taken at school the previous term displayed in a leather frame. Harry must have taken the picture whilst she was in the kitchen, making him his second cup of coffee. It was all too much and Janine found tears blurring her eyes and streaming down her cheeks. She wept for lost happiness and for Tamsyn's lack of a father, she wept for the weak shell of a man Harry had become, so different from the careless, generous, handsome man she had loved and married. She wept for the bleak past and the grey future, both overshadowed by fears; she wept until she could weep no more and then dragged herself upstairs to toss and turn in fitful sleep until she woke tired and unrefreshed early the next morning.

6

Janine found it extremely difficult to give her attention to her work next day. Her mind kept slipping away from the classroom to her encounter with Harry the previous night. She was haunted by his grey face and her brain churned their conversation over and over again. What else could she have said? What else should she have said? Ought she to tell the police he had visited her? Presumably she ought, yet she had said she would not and was indeed loth to set them on Harry's trail. What would she say if they came to visit her? Came to ask if Harry had been there, to tell her to keep watch for him and let them know? She did not know the answers to any of these questions, yet they kept posing and re-posing themselves as the day wore on and she was very relieved at length to dismiss her class and listen to the children's voices die away from the school and playground. But even then there was no time for thought. Tamsyn appeared at her mother's classroom door and said, 'Come on, Mum, or I'll be late.'

For a moment Janine looked blank then she remembered she had told Tamsyn she would take her over to Chariswood today.

'I'll be with you in a minute,' she said. 'You hop into the car, I won't be long.'

Janine did not even want Tamsyn to walk home from school to the cottage alone with the possibility that Harry was still in the area. She did not trust him, she was afraid he would approach the child again and upset her by telling her who he was. After all, he had taken the photograph so he obviously wanted some contact with his unknown daughter, however tenuous. Tamsyn was well adjusted to having no father, never having had one she did not feel the lack, but if she met him and discovered who he was, all that could so easily change.

They drove over to Chariswood and Tamsyn scurried round to the stables where Barrel and Ned would be waiting. There was no sign of Sir Gavin or Lady Hampton so Janine went back home to do some of her chores before fetching Tamsyn for tea.

The telephone was ringing as she walked into the house and as she reached for the receiver she wondered with a twinge of fear if it was Harry. However, it was her mother's voice, almost incoherent with excitement, which babbled down the line. Janine found herself laughing and saying, 'Mother, Mother! Hold it. I can't hear a word! Calm down and start again.'

'Sorry dear, but I'm so excited,' cried her mother. 'I went in for this competition on a corn flakes packet and I've won! I've won a three weeks' cruise in the West Indies over Christmas and New Year. Isn't it marvellous? Can you imagine?'

'Mother, how wonderful!' exclaimed Janine when she was able to get a word in. 'Aren't you clever? What did you have to do?'

Her mother explained the competition and how she had solved the puzzle and written a slogan, but all the time she was speaking, Janine was considering whether to tell her about Harry's appearance. What would her mother say? Would she advise her or merely act as a sounding-board? Was it fair to burden her with it all? She had been a tower of strength when Harry had just gone and continued to be quietly supportive as Janine set about bringing up Tamsyn alone, but now perhaps it was time for Janine to make her own decision, unaided. Anyway her mother was so excited just now, Janine was determined not to spoil the moment by relating last night's visit. Having decided, she turned her full attention back to her mother in time to hear her say, 'The only thing that worries me is that I shan't be able to have Christmas

84

with you and Tam. Will you mind awfully? It'll be the first time on your own for Christmas since Harry left.'

Janine reassured her, 'We'll be fine, Mother, don't worry at all. Yours is a chance in a lifetime. Did you say it was for two?'

'Yes, but I did ask immediately if they'd put Tam in as well as you if we paid for her, but they said no.'

'Don't worry, Mother,' repeated Janine. 'I haven't three weeks school holiday at Christmas anyway, so we couldn't have come. Who are you going to ask?'

'I thought I'd ask Betty, she's on her own too since Edward died,' and Janine's mother went off into the plans she and her friend Betty had already made. By the time her mother finally rang off, promising to come down to Friars Bridge for a few days during the half-term holiday next week, Janine just had time to make and drink a cup of tea before she had to turn out and collect Tamsyn.

This time as she pulled up outside Chariswood, she found Sir Gavin Hampton waiting for her.

'Tamsyn isn't quite ready,' he said as he opened her car door for her, 'come in and have a cup of tea.'

'Thank you,' replied Janine, 'but I've just had one at home.'

'Well, come in anyway,' he insisted. 'I want to talk to you and it's too cold out here.' He led the way in through the front door and installed her in front of the fire in his library.

'If you won't have tea, will you have a drink?' he said. But again she declined and waited while he poured himself a scotch and settled into a chair opposite her.

'I've been up on the hill this afternoon,' he said. 'I was round and about on the slope above Mill Cottage on and off for some time, certainly at the time Tamsyn usually walks over to us, but there was no sign of anyone up there today.'

Janine found that she had been

holding her breath and she let it out slowly with relief as she heard his words. She realised she had been terrified he would have met Harry still lurking among the bushes. Perhaps Harry really had gone away with her ten pounds and Tamsyn's picture in his pocket.

Sir Gavin must have noticed the change in her face although she had tried not to let her emotions show, for he looked at her for a moment and said, 'Is something the matter? Is there anything I can do to help?'

For an instant Janine felt a desperate urge to confide everything to Sir Gavin, but she overcame it and answered hastily, 'No, no. It's just such a relief to know there was no one there. I mean, it must have been coincidence and Tamsyn just happened to see the man twice.' She knew her explanation sounded feeble but she decided if she said any more it would be worse than leaving it at what she had said already. Sir Gavin looked at her intently and asked, 'Are you sure? You seem very jumpy today, has anything gone wrong?'

'No, I'm just tired I expect. I'll be glad when tomorrow's over and we break for half-term. I must say it's been quite a strain settling in to a new house, a new village and a new job.' Then she remembered it was Sir Gavin who had been against her appointment and she added boldly, 'But it's been a challenge and one I've been pleased to accept. I like hard work and I'm doing fine.' Her eyes met his, defying him to disagree with her and he returned her gaze steadily until at last she lowered her eyes. She said with a forced smile, 'Of course it's been a great help to Tamsyn to be able to come here and ride. She's hardly missed her old friends at all; she's been too busy.'

Sir Gavin smiled back and said, 'Well, she's doing very well at her riding, and if she keeps it up she'll soon be winning all the local shows. Janine,' he paused fractionally before going on, 'Janine, call truce. You don't have to defend yourself to me. I'm sorry if I made you feel you had to, I should never have said what I did.' The even tenor of his voice did not change as he spoke, the transition to the use of her Christian name was smooth and almost unnoticed, and for an instant Janine did not take in what he had said; then as his words penetrated, her heart turned over and she looked up sharply to find him watching her with the suspicion of a twinkle lurking deep in his dark and serious eyes. She felt childish colour flood to her cheeks, but she was spared the necessity of answering by Lady Hampton, who came in at that moment saying, 'Ah, there you are. Tamsyn was looking for you, Mrs Sherwood, and we knew you were about somewhere because of the car.'

Janine jumped to her feet and said, 'I'm sorry if she troubled you, Lady Hampton. I'm just coming.'

'There's no hurry, my dear. Mrs Deeben has carried her off to the kitchen for a piece of cake. Have you had some tea?'

'Yes, thank you, Lady Hampton. If you don't mind, I'll retrieve Tamsyn and get on home. There are several things I want to get organised before half-term.'

'Of course, it's half-term next week. Annabel and Caroline are coming down for a couple of days. Perhaps Tamsyn would like to come over and play one day. Or are you going away?'

'That's very kind,' replied Janine. 'We aren't going away, my mother is coming to us for a few days. But I'm sure you won't want Tamsyn here if your grandchildren are coming. They'll want their pony to themselves.'

'I'm sure they'd love her to come,' said Lady Hampton. 'They know so few children round here, certainly none of the right age. I'll give you a ring early next week when we both know what our plans are.'

Unable to do anything else, Janine thanked her and, still avoiding Sir

Gavin's eyes, went to collect Tamsyn from the kitchen. Sir Gavin was waiting by the car when they came out and as he saw them into it, he said, 'I'll keep an eye on that hill for a day or two yet. Perhaps it would be wiser if Tamsyn didn't come that way alone again for a while, just until we're sure he isn't coming back.'

He put his hand on to Janine's arm resting on the car's open window, and said, 'If there's anything I can do to help please ask. Trust me.'

At the touch of his hand Janine felt as if an electric current had passed through her, a violent shock that startled and scared her. She withdrew her arm and closed the window a little so that she had to reply to him through a narrow slit.

'Thank you,' she said, her voice strangely calm while her mind whirled. 'If I need any help I'll ask. Goodbye.' She wound up the window and with Tamsyn waving cheerfully, they drove off down the drive.

Later that evening when Tamsyn was safely asleep in bed and she had time to think, Janine reviewed her conversation with Sir Gavin. She recognised and acknowledged how strongly attracted to him she was, but she also bore in mind the promise she had made to herself when Harry had deserted her; 'I will never, never become dependent on any man again. From this moment I rely entirely on myself.' The thought of turning to Sir Gavin for advice on what she should do about Harry's visit was extremely tempting; surely he would know what to do, how to act; but she had resisted the temptation to tell him this evening and was determined to continue to do so. Her battles were her own and with her usual well-tried courage she was resolute in her decision to fight alone. Sir Gavin Hampton and such temptations must be avoided from now on until the situation had been resolved in some way. Even then, she admitted to herself, it would probably be wiser to keep her visits to Chariswood to a minimum.

The jangle of the phone broke into her thoughts and with the two men on her mind Janine was surprised to find her mother on the line again.

'Janine? It's Mum.'

'Hallo Mum. Won another competition?' There was laughter in her voice and relief that it was only her mother; but her mother remained serious.

'I thought you ought to know Harry's mother died today. She's been ill for some time in hospital, they'd been expecting it, and she just slipped away this afternoon.'

'Oh.' Janine could think of nothing to say, but her mother did not speak so she added, 'I see, thank you for telling me, Mother.'

'I heard it by accident this evening when I met Mrs James who'd been visiting her aunt in the same ward.'

'Well, thank you for letting me know, Mother. Do you think I should come up for the funeral? I suppose it'll be early next week. I'll be on half-term.'

As if Janine had not spoken her mother continued, 'It really was most peculiar. Harry's been there, to see her and he was with a policeman. He talked to his mother, behind the screens you know, and the policeman stood outside. They'd brought him from prison and do you know, he suddenly slipped out between the screens, bolted to the fire door, one of those push-bar things, and made off down the fire escape. The policeman, or warder, or whoever he was, chased him, but he got away; the man didn't catch him. They came to the ward again to ask Harry's mother where he might go, but she had slid back into unconsciousness. Did you know he was in prison, Janine?'

Janine was shaken by her mother's account of Harry's escape and she had to rally herself to say, 'I — er — I had heard; yes, Mother.'

'But darling, why didn't you tell me?

How did you find out?'

'I — er — heard it on the grape-vine,' said Janine vaguely. 'I expect that's why his mother stopped coming to see us. She must have known and was afraid we'd ask questions or something.' Again Janine had to fight hard against the urge to admit Harry's visit to her mother, but she was still uncertain as to what her mother's reaction would be and she bit back the confession, saying instead, 'Do you think I should go to the funeral? I don't want to see Harry.'

'I should think he's most unlikely to be there in the circumstances,' replied her mother.

'I suppose so,' sighed Janine.

'Look, darling,' said Mrs Watson, 'I suggest you come up for the funeral on Tuesday and we'll go together. I feel I must go too, and it'll be easier for us both if we go together; then I'll come down for the rest of the week as planned. Can you get Tamsyn looked after for the day? I don't think she should come, do you?'

'I expect I can,' said Janine. 'She's quite friendly with several people now. I suppose you're right. That's the best thing for me to do.'

7

Everything proved remarkably easy to arrange as it turned out. She told Tamsyn the next morning of the death of her grandmother and found that the little girl had only vague recollections of the old lady who visited them occasionally.

'We hadn't seen her for a long time,' explained Janine, 'but I must go to her funeral.'

'Am I coming too?' asked Tamsyn.

'No, darling, I don't think so. Gran's coming with me and then we're both coming back down here for the rest of half-term. I'll only be away for one day. I thought perhaps you could go to Sarah's or Susan's for the day. I'll fix something up over the weekend.'

But Tamsyn had other ideas and while she was at Chariswood for her riding after school, she went to see

Lady Hampton, so that when Janine arrived later to fetch her, she found Tamsyn had been invited there for the whole of Tuesday, and indeed for the Monday night.

'It'll mean you can go up to your mother's the night before and not have to dash there and back in the one day,' said Lady Hampton. 'Far too much driving in one day, specially if you've attended a funeral in the middle. I'm sorry to hear of your mother-in-law's death.'

'I understand she'd been ill for some-time,' said Janine. 'We'd almost lost touch — just Christmas cards, you know. The situation was rather awkward.'

'Of course,' sympathised Lady Hampton. 'However, if it would suit you, Tamsyn could come for tea on Monday, sleep the night and you could collect her when you get back on Tuesday evening. Annabel and Caroline will be here so she'll have them to play with.'

Janine had been going to refuse any

invitation that came for Tamsyn from Chariswood over half-term, feeling that she was already there far too often, but it certainly did facilitate her arrangements to accept now and so she found herself expressing her thanks and promising to bring Tamsyn over on Monday afternoon.

Janine spent Monday evening in the familiar surroundings of her mother's house in a suburb of London. Its very familiarity gave Janine a sense of comfortable safety which she had not enjoyed in the last few days, ever since Harry had appeared on her doorstep. It was the house where she had grown up and as she lay in her old bed, counting the rosette patterns on the wallpaper as she always had done, it was as if she had been transported back through time to the days before Harry had come into her life, when her father had been alive and things had been so easy. Her mother had spoiled her tonight, bringing her a hot drink in bed, recognising there was something worrying her, yet having the good sense not to question, merely to wait until at last it all came flooding out. These tactics had never failed in the past and she had no reason to suppose they would now; if not tonight, then during her stay at Friars Bridge.

It was raining next day and in the grey dampness the two women drove to St David's church. There were few mourners, just themselves and three others, two more women and a man who stood well apart. The service was short and all through it Janine found herself probing the shadowy corners of the church, half expecting to see Harry's pale face; but he did not come and soon they were outside in the drizzle once more, standing at the graveside. As she watched them lower the coffin into the dank ground, Janine felt a deep regret that she had not maintained contact with Harry's mother, and yet again she glanced round to see if he was there, but could see no sign of him.

They made their way back to the car and were just getting in, when the man who had attended the funeral approached them. He spoke to Janine.

Mrs Sherwood? I'm Sergeant Harrington, CID. I'm making enquiries into the escape from police custody of your husband, Harold James Sherwood, while visiting his mother at St Margaret's Hospital.'

'This is it!' thought Janine in panic. 'I should have known the police would be here. He's going to ask me if I've seen Harry. What do I say?' However, despite her turmoil of mind she spoke to him calmly.

'My ex-husband, Sergeant. We are no longer married and haven't been for several years.' The policeman nodded.

'Of course. You know why he did not attend his mother's funeral, however.' It was a statement not a question and Janine admitted that she did. Her mother, who had been standing listening to their conversation, spoke then.

'She knows all that because I told

her. She's had no contact with Harry since he walked out on her. She only knew that her mother-in-law had died because I told her. Coming today was merely a matter of respect on both our parts.'

'And you are — ?'

'I'm Mary Watson, Mrs Sherwood's mother.'

'I see,' said the sergeant. 'Well, as you know, Harry escaped while visiting his mother in hospital. He had compassionate parole to go and see her because she was dying. Anyway, to cut a long story short, we have reason to believe he may be in some danger, so if he does try to contact you, perhaps you'd get in touch with me here.' He gave Janine a slip of paper with his name and a telephone number pencilled on it. His eyes held hers for a long moment.

'Don't shield him through a misguided sense of loyalty, it wouldn't be doing him any favours,' he said. 'Agreed he'll have to go back to prison, but finishing his stretch is not the only reason we want him back.'

'He walked out of my life seven years ago, Sergeant, leaving me with an unborn baby and a mountain of debts. I can assure you he's not going to find a welcome waiting if he does decide to contact me again. I haven't even told him where I am.' Janine chose her words with extreme care so that she told no lie yet did not reveal Harry had already been to her. She knew she ought to tell the sergeant at once and yet at the back of her mind she heard herself promising Harry that she would not go to the police.

'Don't worry, Sergeant,' said Mrs Watson heartily, 'any sign of Harry and you'll be the first to know.'

'Thank you madam,' he said. 'Good day to you both.' And he disappeared into the wet London street.

Janine and Mrs Watson got into the car, glad to be out of the rain. As she drew out into the traffic, Mrs Watson said casually, 'Why didn't you tell him that Harry had been to see you already?'

Janine stared at her mother in amazement.

'How did you know he had?' she said, relieved it was out at last.

Her mother laughed. 'I've known you all your life, darling. I can always tell when you're lying, your ears go pink.'

'I didn't lie to him!' protested Janine.

'Only by omission,' pointed out her mother.

'I couldn't have helped him much anyway,' sighed Janine. 'Harry was frightened. He said he was in danger, that some gang of criminals was out to kill him. He said he wasn't even safe from them in prison and that they'd get him there. I tell you, Mother, he was really afraid. He wanted me to hide him until he'd made some arrangements or other; to get out of the country, I suppose. But I couldn't help him, I couldn't risk Tam, either physically if Harry did have people after him, or mentally in case he told her, or she guessed, who he was.'

'That was wise of you, the turning

him out, I mean. You don't want to get involved with him again; there's no future for you there. And if he's really in trouble, your job is to protect Tamsyn.' They were words Janine was to remember in days to come, but at this moment she did not realise their full significance.

'But I do understand you couldn't give him up to the police, either,' Mrs Watson went on. 'I would have if it had been up to me, but you always had a soft centre no matter how hard you've managed to grow your outer shell.'

'He took Tam's picture from the mantelpiece.'

'Poor man.' But Mrs Watson's voice held no pity. 'If he comes again, Janine, you must tell the police. One chance is enough.' Then, as if she had decided they had spent enough time on her erst-while son-in-law, she said, 'Are we fetching Tam from her friends' house this evening?'

Janine tore her thoughts away from Harry and the police and answered,

'Yes, she's been there quite long enough. It's the place where she goes riding. She almost lives there as it is.'

'Come on then,' said Mrs Watson. 'Let's collect our luggage and drive down and fetch her.'

By the time they pulled up in front of Chariswood, it was growing dark and the light in the porch shone a welcome in the gloom.

'What a beautiful house,' said Mrs Watson in admiration, 'a mixture, but none the less lovely for that.'

Mrs Deeben opened the front door and led them through to the drawing-room. As they crossed the hall, hoots of laughter came from behind the dining-room door, and Tamsyn's voice was heard amid the others. Janine paused, about to go in there, but Mrs Deeben said, 'Lady Hampton and Mrs Meredith are in the drawing-room.' She opened the door saying, 'Mrs Sherwood, madam.' She stood aside to let Janine and her mother pass her and then closed the door behind them.

106

Lady Hampton was sitting by the fire and a woman, so like Sir Gavin that it was obvious she was his sister, sat opposite her. Both got up as Janine entered the room, Lady Hampton saying as she rose, 'Janine, my dear. How did it go? Tamsyn's been as good as gold, it's been a pleasure to have her. You don't know my daughter, do you? Sandra, this is Janine Sherwood, Tamsyn's mother.'

Janine introduced her mother and they were drawn to the fire to warm themselves.

'The children are just finishing tea in the dining-room, they'll be in in a minute. Gavin's in charge which accounts for the noise.' They all laughed at that and Lady Hampton added, 'Mrs Deeben'll tell them you're here.'

Sandra began to chat to Janine, saying how easily Tamsyn had got on with Annabel and Caroline.

'Although my two are a bit older, they really played well together. Annabel mothered her a bit, well, they both did, but Tamsyn didn't seem to mind and she is very mature for her age; well able to hold her own with them.'

The noise from the dining-room suddenly increased as the children erupted into the hall and on into the drawing-room, followed by Sir Gavin who was still laughing and saying, 'I thought I was entertaining three young ladies to tea, but they were more like three amazons!' Tamsyn had run to hug her mother and Janine said, 'I hope you've been behaving yourself, Tamsyn.'

'Oh, I was,' cried Tamsyn, 'but Uncle Gavin was so funny, he was showing us how to turn a plate of stewed plums right round without spilling any of them, only he got stuck and all the juice ran up his sleeve.' All three girls dissolved into giggles again and Sir Gavin said ruefully, 'We weren't going to tell your mothers about that if you remember!'

'And Uncle Gavin says Tam can come over again tomorrow to play,' piped up the younger of the other two girls, Caroline. She was not much older than Tamsyn and her blonde curls and blue eyes made her look angelic, but there was mischief lurking behind the innocence as she turned the full blast of her charm on her uncle, 'Didn't you, Uncle Gavin?'

'Only if Mrs Sherwood says she may. Her grandmother has come to stay and they may be busy.'

Remembering her manners suddenly, Janine introduced her mother to Sir Gavin.

'Did everything go well?' asked Sir Gavin, as they shook hands.

'There weren't many there,' said Janine. 'I'm glad I went.' She was about to go on and say how grateful she was to them for having Tamsyn when she was horrified to hear her mother say, 'The police were there though, looking for Harry.'

Janine looked at her aghast and hissed, 'Mother!'

There was a sudden silence and Annabel asked, 'Who's Harry?'

'Just a man Mrs Sherwood knows,' replied Sir Gavin evenly. 'Now will you go and help Tamsyn get her luggage? Bring it downstairs and we'll put it in the car. Mrs Sherwood wants to be off.'

The children went upstairs happily and an awkward silence descended on the drawing-room. Janine broke it by saying brightly, 'You're right, we must get back. Thank you again for having Tamsyn.'

They all went into the hall and Sir Gavin picked up Tamsyn's little case and carried it out to the car. It was quite dark by now and the only light came from the porch. Tamsyn and her grandmother climbed into the car while Janine stowed the suitcase in the boot. Sir Gavin spoke softly, 'You mustn't let what your mother said worry you. Tamsyn didn't take it in, I'm sure.'

'I hope not,' replied Janine tightly, promising herself a few words with her mother when they were alone.

Tamsyn stuck her head out of the window and called, 'Bye-bye, Uncle

Gavin. Thank you for a lovely time.'

As they drove off down the drive, Janine asked her daughter, 'Who told you to call Sir Gavin, uncle?'

'He did,' replied Tamsyn, surprised. 'He said Annabel and Caroline did, so it would be easier if I did as well.'

Later that evening when Tamsyn was safely in bed and they were alone, Janine tackled her mother.

'How could you?' she cried, 'in front of Tam is bad enough, I certainly don't want her to know her father is a convict; but I don't want anyone else to know either, it'll surely get back to her and it won't do either of us any good.'

Her mother looked contrite. 'I'm sorry, darling, I am really,' she said. 'It's just that the whole incident's been preying on my mind and I spoke without consideration. But listen, I've been thinking, Janine, suppose that man wasn't the police but one of the gang who are looking for Harry? Suppose he just said he was a policeman? We didn't ask him for identification, did we? We didn't see his card, or whatever it is they're meant to show.'

'No,' agreed Janine slowly, her mind diverted for a moment from her anger. 'But surely he wouldn't dare approach us like that if he wasn't police. I mean we could have asked to see his warrant card.'

'We could,' acknowledged her mother, 'but we didn't and that's what's worrying me.'

'He gave me a phone number to ring,' pointed out Janine. 'It must be a police station.' She crossed to the telephone and taking from her handbag the paper she had been given, she dialled the number on it. After a moment a voice answered.

'Hallo.'

'Hallo,' said Janine, 'is that the police station?'

'No,' came the reply. 'Who wants to know? Who is that?'

Janine replaced the receiver. In the

silence that followed she turned to her mother pale-faced. 'It wasn't a police station,' she whispered. 'Thank God I didn't give that man any information.'

8

The rest of half-term passed peacefully enough, although there was an unusual tension between Janine and her mother. Both were worried by the state of affairs for different reasons. Janine was afraid that whoever was after Harry might take some action against herself, or worse still, Tamsyn, to gain information of his whereabouts; and her mother was afraid that Harry was going to become involved yet again in Janine's life, just when it seemed her future was assured with a good job that she enjoyed and a comfortable home in which to bring up Tamsyn. However, by mutual consent neither referred to Harry or Sergeant Harrington again and when Mrs Watson returned to her own home again on Sunday afternoon, each felt a secret relief at being away from the other for a while, to allow time for them to forget their differences and resume their normal easy relationship.

During the days of half-term, Janine found herself looking over her shoulder, watching to see if she was being followed. When considering this rationally she felt it was stupid, but fear was established and she could not quite rid herself of the need to look behind her. However, once she was back at school and she knew Tamsyn was safely in the confines of the school buildings, she relaxed a little and her mind was too occupied to allow her time for very much thought about Harry. Occasionally a thought intruded, but she always pushed it firmly to the back of her mind and turned her attention to more immediate things; the school nativity play, the junior girls' netball team, or the shoplifting charge against one of her seven-year old boys and his six-year old sister. She heard nothing from Harry and gradually her fears began to recede; so that when she and Tamsyn went to spend the weekend with Mrs Watson just before she set off on her winter cruise, Janine was far more relaxed and at ease than she had been since the day of the funeral and she and her mother both enjoyed their weekend together as much as they always had.

Tamsyn continued to ride at Chariswood every weekend, but had gone there less often after school as Janine was still unwilling to let her walk across the hill alone. The little girl thought this was stupid, but Janine remained adamant on the subject. However, she drove her over there two afternoons a week and watched her daughter's progress with pride. Occasionally Sir Gavin or his mother would join her by the paddock to watch. At first Janine feared some comment would be made about her mother's remark concerning the police, but neither of them referred to it again and gradually Janine relaxed there too, finding pleasure in the company of both Lady Hampton and her son.

It was returning from one of

Tamsyn's riding sessions towards the very end of the term that Janine found Sergeant Harrington waiting in a car outside her house. She saw the car as she drove up, but it was only as they got out that she realised who it was.

'Tamsyn,' she cried, 'get back into the car.' Tamsyn stared at her in amazement. 'In the car? Where are we going?'

'Just get in,' said Janine urgently, 'and lock the doors.'

'Mrs Sherwood. I've been waiting for you,' said Sergeant Harrington walking across to where her car was parked. 'I'd like a word with you alone if you don't mind.'

'Why? What do you want?' All Janine's fears came flooding back as the man approached, and she backed up against the door of her car in case Tamsyn had not locked it.

'We'd be more comfortable inside the house, don't you think?' He stopped in surprise as he saw her backing away from him and said, 'Is something the matter?'

'Leave me alone. Go away or I'll call the police, do you hear?'

'But I am the police. Remember? I spoke to you at your mother-in-law's funeral. Sergeant Harrington.'

'I don't believe you. Show me your warrant card or whatever it's called.'

'All right,' he said calmly. 'It's in my inside pocket. I'm going to put my hand in now and get it out. O.K.?'

Janine nodded uncertainly, the preposterous idea that he might draw a gun flitting through her mind. The man slipped his hand into his jacket pocket, withdrew his identification card and held it out to Janine. She looked at it carefully before she said, 'All right, we'd better go indoors.' She opened the car door for Tamsyn to get out and all three of them went into the house. Once inside, Janine sent Tamsyn into the living room to watch television and she took Sergeant Harrington into the kitchen.

'If you're really a policeman why

wasn't the number you gave me to ring a police station?' she demanded.

'Did you ring it?'

'I rang but they said it wasn't a police station.'

'What did they say?'

'I rang off. I thought you might be one of the men after Harry.'

'I see. Well, I'm with the drugs squad and the number I gave you put you through to a special unit. If you'd asked to speak to me I'd have been found or would have called you back as soon as I could.'

'They might have explained,' said Janine defensively.

'We have to be a little careful who we reveal ourselves to,' pointed out the sergeant. 'Why did you ring? Did your husband make contact?'

Janine decided not to answer that question, parrying it with one of her own.

'Why have you come here?'

'I'm afraid I have some bad news for you. A body has been found at

Felixstowe; it's Harry Sherwood. He's been shot.'

Janine stared at him in horror. 'Harry's dead?' she whispered. 'Oh God.'

The policeman pulled forward a kitchen chair and Janine collapsed on to it, her legs too weak to hold her.

At that moment the doorbell rang, but Janine felt quite unable to move and made no effort to get up to answer it. The sergeant turned to do so, but Tamsyn beat him to it.

'It's Uncle Gavin,' she called. 'Mum's in the kitchen with a man,' she went on, turning back to Sir Gavin, 'I'm watching television.' Sir Gavin came through to the kitchen and with one look at Janine's pale and stricken face said, 'What's going on? Janine, you look dreadful. Whatever is the matter?'

'It's Harry,' she replied in a low voice. 'He's been shot. He's dead.'

'Who are you?' demanded Sir Gavin, turning to the policeman. The sergeant explained and then returning his attention to Janine asked, 'Did he come to see you? Why didn't you tell me?'

'He came before you asked me about him,' answered Janine wearily.

'It's a great pity you did not tell me then, perhaps we could have saved him.'

'But I didn't know where he was! All I did was give him ten pounds and a meal,' cried Janine.

'I think we could leave the questions for a while,' interposed Sir Gavin. 'You need a drink. What is there?'

Janine looked at him blankly for a moment and then said, 'Nothing much.'

'Tea then,' and Sir Gavin switched on the kettle. 'We'll get Tamsyn to bed and then, Sergeant, we can sort all this out. There is no immediate hurry I presume?'

Recognising the voice of authority, the sergeant, who had been about to protest, said, 'No, sir.'

Sir Gavin took over then. He made tea for Janine and sent her to lie down in her room; he cooked eggs and bacon for Tamsyn, telling her that her mother was not feeling well, and then read to her before tucking her into bed.

'Did you know Mummy wasn't well?' asked Tamsyn as he kissed her good-night. 'Is that why you came?'

'No, she wasn't telling anyone. I came over because you left your coat in the stables and I thought you might need it for school in the morning. I've left it downstairs on the hall stand. Don't worry, I'm sure she'll be feeling better in the morning.'

'How did you know Harry had been here?' Janine asked the sergeant when they had gathered together again in the living-room. The man put his hand in his pocket and drew out a crumpled photograph. It was the one of Tamsyn which Harry had removed from the mantlepiece.

'When we found him it was all he had on him. His pockets had been emptied. Now, suppose we have the whole story.'

Janine recounted her evening with

Harry, and the sergeant and Sir Gavin listened without interruption until she had finished.

'And if I'd told you all this before, he might still be alive, in prison, but at least alive.' There was anguish in her voice.

'I must say that is possibly true,' admitted the policeman, 'but from what you say it confirms our suspicions that Harry was in some danger wherever he was. He had something or knew something which made him a risk to the rest of the mob. Something worth killing for. He didn't leave anything with you for safe-keeping, did he? A package, a letter or something? Did he mention any names?' Janine shook her head.

'Well, if you think of anything, let me know.'

'There is one thing,' she said suddenly. 'Harry did say they thought he'd informed on them, before he was caught himself. Perhaps it was just plain revenge.'

'Certainly someone helped the police several years ago when we picked up a whole section of the organisation. If that was Harry, and they'd discovered it, I'm not surprised he was afraid.'

'Don't you know who the informer was?' asked Janine amazed.

'No, it was an anonymous tip-off. We get them sometimes when the person's too scared to come forward and get involved, or already too involved to come forward.'

Janine shuddered. 'It's all horrible. Frightening and horrible.'

'I'm afraid we shall have to ask you to come and do a formal identification, Mrs Sherwood.'

'I can't leave here now, I mean it's the last day of term, tomorrow. I have to be here. Where do I have to go? You said he was at Felixtowe? Why was he there, of all places?'

'Trying to leave the country inconspicuously, I should imagine.'

'I'll drive you over there,' offered Sir Gavin. 'You can leave Tamsyn at

Chariswood for the day and night too, if necessary. It's a long way to go.' He did not make this as a suggestion, but as a definite arrangement. 'That'll be all right, won't it, Sergeant?'

The sergeant nodded. 'If you'd like to take Mrs Sherwood to the police station at Felixstowe they'll be expecting her.'

He left then, Sir Gavin seeing him out of the house while Janine, still in a state of shock, sat immobile in her chair. When Sir Gavin came back into the room he said gently, 'You should try and get some sleep. There's nothing more you can do till tomorrow and you've got to get through the final day at school.' His gentleness was her undoing and Janine's tears fell unchecked. Sir Gavin put his arms round her and let her weep. He said nothing, but the strength of his arms brought comfort and as her sobs died away, he proffered a large white handkerchief, then drew away from her and began to mend the fire, leaving her to regain her self-possession. When he turned to her again she had done so, and she said quietly, 'I'm sorry, I just can't get it out of mind that if I'd told the police about Harry they might have found him before — before the others did.'

'Was it Harry on the hill, who spoke to Tamsyn?'

'Yes, I should have told you, but I was afraid.'

'Never be afraid to tell me anything. Trust me, I'll always help.' His gentle tone was replaced by a brisker one and he said, 'Now, go to bed. The day after term ends bring Tamsyn over to Chariswood. She can sleep the night and we'll go to Felixstowe and get things sorted out. All right?'

Janine nodded, unable to think of a better plan. If only her mother were not away she would have given Janine moral support and Janine would not have had to rely on the kindness of the Hamptons; but her mother was already on her cruise and Janine did not want to go to identify Harry's body alone, so she said wearily, 'Yes, thank you, Sir Gavin.'

'Janine, couldn't you drop the 'sir'? You know me well enough for that surely.'

'Yes, Gavin,' she said meekly. She was too tired to argue. He gave a brief nod of satisfaction and, after warning her to lock up after him, left her to dose herself with aspirin and go to bed.

9

How Janine got through the next day she was not sure. She had slept badly and her eyes were ringed with tiredness, but there was no let-up on the last day of the Christmas Term. The school positively bubbled with excitement as the walls were cleared, pictures and models were packed into carrier bags and the final assembly, taken by the vicar, reminded them all of what Christmas was really about. The children sang their carols, collected their accumulated luggage and, bright-eyed, bid noisy farewell to the teachers before going home. Janine felt her smile was fixed to her face, but in the general hubbub her tension passed unnoticed and in the strange quiet which followed the departure of the last child, she collapsed behind her office desk, relieved to have completed her first term. She was pleased with the start she had made and with the relationship she had established with children, staff and parents; but her feeling of satisfaction was only momentarily enjoyed before the horrible events of the previous evening crowded in on her again and, sighing, she collected her things together and joined Tamsyn in the car.

As they arrived home they heard the telephone ringing, and Tamsyn rushed to answer it.

'It's a man for you,' she said.

It was Sergeant Harrington to tell her that the inquest on Harry had been set for the day after she was coming to Felixstowe. He asked her if she could stay over for it as they would need her evidence of identification.

'Yes,' she said wearily, 'I'll stay.'

It meant she had to ring Gavin and tell him the change of plan.

'Don't worry,' he reassured her. 'We'll stay as long as necessary. I'll book us in somewhere over there. Leave it to me. Mother is delighted Tamsyn's coming and my sister and the girls will be down in a day or so.'

'I don't mean to be away long,' began Janine, but Gavin said, 'Tamsyn's welcome to stay as long as it takes.' And Janine was grateful.

The Sherwoods drove to Chariswood the next morning. It was a bright day, alight with pale winter sun. Tamsyn could not wait to go and find Ned and Barrel and as soon as she had said hallo to Lady Hampton she was fidgeting to be off.

'You're in the same bedroom as last time, Tamsyn dear,' said Lady Hampton. 'Of course Annabel and Caroline aren't here this time, but they'll be down in a few days for Christmas. Go and change and then run along and find Ned.'

Tamsyn needed no second bidding and with a quick hug for Janine, she vanished upstairs to put on her jodhpurs.

Lady Hampton turned to Janine.

'Poor Sandra; Michael, her husband, is still in the Mid East, and isn't due back until the end of January. Gavin won't be long now, he had to go over to one of the farms earlier, a chimney collapsed through a roof, but he should be back any minute. Mrs Deeben'll bring us a cup of coffee while we wait,' and she led the way into the sunny drawing-room.

Gavin arrived before the coffee and joined them for a quick cup after he had stowed Janine's case in the boot of the car with his own. Then they were off on the long journey to Felixstowe.

They spoke little on the way at first, each busy with his own thoughts; Janine was trying to prepare herself mentally for seeing Harry dead, and Gavin, respecting her troubled mind, kept quiet and perfected a plan he and his mother had devised for Christmas.

They stopped for lunch at a pub by a river and sat in the little dining-room by the window, watching the water slide by under arching willows. The sun had disappeared and an all-pervading greyness, more in keeping with Janine's mood, slid across the sky. Before long they were on the road again and at last, driving through misty drizzle, they reached the port of Felixstowe.

Pale and nervous, Janine entered the police station with Gavin behind her. Together they were taken to the mortuary and there, lying on a table, was a white-sheeted figure. The sheet was drawn back from the face and unconciously clutching tight hold of Gavin's hand, Janine stepped forward to look.

Harry lay cold and peaceful, his eyes closed and the lines of fear smoothed from his face. Despite a grey stubble round his chin, he looked younger than when she had last seen him. He looked asleep. For a moment Janine studied him, almost unemotionally. It was if this strange cold corpse had little to do with the Harry she had both loved and hated. As when he had visited her at Friars Bridge that night, she found she felt neither emotion now, only pity for his weakness and sorrow for his death.

She nodded to the policeman who had come with them and said in a low voice, 'That's him. That's Harry Sherwood, my husband.'

Quietly they left the cold body to the cold room and promising to be at the inquest at ten o'clock next morning, went out into the December dusk. A wind had sprung up, but it was not because of this that Janine drew her coat more closely round her and shivered.

'Come on, let's find somewhere warm for a drink.' Gavin took her arm and led her unresisting into a pub a little further down the road.

The warmth of the lounge bar enveloped them as they pushed through the swing doors and the jangle of music coming through from the public-bar juke box heightened the contrast between the warm friendliness of the pub and the cold silence of the mortuary.

Gavin bought them each a brandy and they sat on an old settle beside the glowing coals of an open fire.

'Thank you for coming with me,' Janine said simply. The fire was bringing back colour to her cheeks and gradually easing the chill which had invaded her as she looked down at Harry so cold and still.

'It's not something I'd have liked to do on my own either,' admitted Gavin, 'whoever it was.'

'It's the finality of it all,' went on Janine. 'I mean, it brings you up short when someone you know, someone about your own age, dies. You suddenly realise how precious life is and just how much you can waste it even though you can never be sure how much time you have yourself.'

Perhaps it was the brandy, but suddenly Janine felt the need to unburden herself and once she started to speak the words flooded out, tumbling over each other; and without saying a single word Gavin sat nursing his brandy, swirling it gently in its balloon, watching it catch the firelight as he listened, and by listening halved the burden of her cares.

'I haven't loved Harry for years. It was as if part of me had been amputated when he left, and then gradually the wound healed, the rest of me adjusted to the loss. The terrible pain subsided to a dull ache and then even that faded away. It was a shock when he came back the other day, but really there was no pain. And when he left and I knew I wouldn't see him again, I didn't mind; but seeing him there today, it was so final. Poor Tamsyn. She'll never have the chance to know her father now. He took her picture, you know. I didn't want her to see him or to know who he was, but perhaps I was wrong about that too. Perhaps I should have left that decision to her. Only I left it too late. She's remarkably incurious about her father, but will she always be? Was I right to deny her the chance to meet him when the occasion arose? She's only seven now, what does she know? But when she's seventeen and is seeking her identity?' Suddenly she laughed self-consciously and said awkwardly, 'Sorry, boring.'

Gavin smiled at her and said gently, 'No, therapeutic.'

Silence enfolded them for a moment but was rudely shattered by a guffaw from the public bar.

'Another drink?' asked Gavin, 'Or shall we find somewhere to eat?'

'Eat, please,' replied Janine, suddenly feeling hungry. 'I'd love a steak and chips.'

'You're on,' agreed Gavin cheerfully. 'Let's go.' In spite of the sombre reason for their journey, they both enjoyed the rest of the evening and returned to their hotel early enough for Janine to have a good night's sleep in preparation for the inquest next day.

She did not feel like eating breakfast

in the morning, but Gavin insisted that she at least have a slice of toast and some coffee before they left for the coroner's court. By the time they took their places she was pale and tense and once again grateful for the steadying presence of Gavin Hampton by her side.

In the event the inquest lasted less than half an hour, with little evidence offered apart from Janine's evidence of identification and a doctor's statement as to the cause of death. Then it was all adjourned while the police continued their investigations, and with a strange feeling of anti-climax they were out in the wintry sun once again. Janine had been told she could make the arrangements for Harry's funeral now, and she and Gavin discussed what to do over a coffee.

'I'd like him put beside his mother,' said Janine. 'There's nowhere else he wanted to go.'

Once she had reached her decisions she was amazed by the speed with which Gavin put them into action and by early afternoon the funeral was arranged at the same London church as old Mrs Sherwood's for two days' time.

'How would it be if we stayed in London until after the funeral?' suggested Gavin suddenly.

'What?' Janine was startled. 'I couldn't. What about Tamsyn?'

'She'll be happy as a sandboy at Chariswood,' replied Gavin. 'I'll give my mother a ring and see if she minds.'

'You can't saddle Lady Hampton with a seven-year old for another two days. It's nearly Christmas and she's sure to be busy.'

'Sandra'll be there with Annabel and Caroline; Mother'll never notice the extra one. You could finish your Christmas shopping in London while you wait.'

But Janine was adamant. 'I must go home,' she said. 'I don't want to leave Tam for too long, even though she loves Chariswood.' She looked seriously at

Gavin and said softly, 'There's something else, Gavin. I want to go to Harry's funeral alone. If you'll have Tamsyn for the day on the actual day, I'd be extremely grateful, but I shall go to London by myself.'

'Of course we'll have her,' he answered, but made no comment on her determination to attend the funeral alone.

Janine said her final goodbye to Harry standing cold and almost alone at the windswept graveside just a few feet from where she had stood so recently in respect for his mother. As she turned away from the grave she was aware of somebody following her, approaching her perhaps. She did not wait to discover, she quickened her step to the cemetery gate, hailed a passing taxi and was swept away from the silence of death to the noisy reality of the London world. It was two days until Christmas, and Janine suddenly felt free as if a great weight had been raised from her shoulders, at last leaving her freed from the shadow of Harry. Tamsyn was at home waiting, bubbling with excitement as Christmas drew near and Janine longed to be with her. This would be their best Christmas yet, she determined, this would be a Christmas they would always remember; and indeed she was right though not in the way she anticipated. Her freedom from the shadow of Harry was to be short-lived.

When she arrived at Chariswood to fetch Tamsyn she was greeted by an ecstatic little girl.

'Mummy, Mummy, Annabel and Caroline have asked if we can come here on Christmas Day. Can we, Mummy? Can we come? Do say we can! It'll be such fun all of us together. Gran won't be coming to us, will she? So couldn't we come? Annabel and Caroline's dad isn't coming too, so we can all cheer each other up. Do say we can, Mummy!'

Janine was rather more than disconcerted by this outburst, and she spoke quite sharply. 'Tamsyn, don't be silly, it's quite out of the question.'

Tamsyn stopped short and her face fell, 'But Mum . . . '

'I'm sorry, Tamsyn, but we're having our Christmas together at home.' Her voice dropped to a harsh whisper, 'We can't intrude here. For goodness sake, child, we'll have a lovely Christmas, just as we always do.'

'Gran's not coming.' Tamsyn's face was mutinous.

As she overcame her initial shock, Janine regained her composure and her voice softened. 'I know she's not, darling, but even so we'll have a lovely day.'

'It'd be more fun here,' replied Tamsyn, unrepentant, and added with unconsidered truth, 'for you as much as for me. There'd be people of my age and people of your age.'

'Can't say fairer than that,' remarked Sandra, emerging from the drawing-room to invite Janine to join them for a drink.

Janine flushed, angry that her exchange with Tamsyn had been overheard, and seeing her embarrassment, Sandra laid a hand on her arm.

'We're all hoping you'll join us for Christmas Day, it'll be a bit flat for my girls with their father away. Pity Arabs don't celebrate Christmas,' she sighed, 'but there it is, and if Tam were here they'd probably play so well that Annabel and Caroline wouldn't miss their father so much, and Tamsyn wouldn't miss her grandmother.'

Janine looked at her and said, 'What about you?' Sandra returned her look and replied simply, 'I'll miss Michael whoever's here.' Then she smiled and said, 'but we really would all love you to come; particularly Mother. She loves a housefull over Christmas and always regrets the old days when the place was crammed with uncles and cousins and aunts. Don't decide now if you don't want to, but don't discard the idea too quickly because I'm sure we'd all enjoy it.' She turned and led Janine into the drawing-room where her mother was waiting.

There was no sign of Gavin and he did not reappear before Janine left for home with Tamsyn. The question of Christmas Day was not referred to again and so was unresolved as they drove home. Tamsyn did not actually mention it aloud, but treated her mother to beseeching and resentful looks by turns until Janine was glad to switch out the light of her daughter's bedroom.

She sat downstairs in the flickering firelight nursing a glass of whisky from a bottle to which she had treated herself, and brooded on her day. The silence was complete and she suddenly realised that the clock had stopped. She crossed the room, rewound it and set it going, her thoughts echoing to its tick, 'Go, stay, go, stay,' when suddenly the telephone shrilled and her musing ceased. It was Lady Hampton on the line.

'I don't want you to feel yourself

under pressure, my dear,' she said, 'but we would love you and Tamsyn to come if you can. The girls have been on at me all evening. But I shall quite understand if you'd rather have a quiet family Christmas with Tamsyn.'

Perhaps it was the word 'family' or a sudden recollection of Tamsyn's pleading eyes, but Janine sighed and made her decision.

'Thank you, Lady Hampton, we'd love to join you on Christmas Day.'

She was rewarded by a whoop of delight from the doorway and turned to find Tamsyn in her nightie standing, listening unashamedly to her mother's telephone conversation. The child's eyes were alight with excitement and Janine felt a wave of love for her. Really she had asked so little and Janine had been about to deny her for the sake of her own pride. She finished her conversation with Lady Hampton and turned with open arms to the little girl in the white nightie standing half-poised for flight upstairs. Tamsyn rushed to hug her and said, 'Are we really going? Mummy, that's brilliant. Tomorrow we can get their presents, can't we?' Janine pressed her face into Tamsyn's soft fair hair.

'Of course we can; and you must decorate our own tree. We're a bit behind this year, but we'll do it tomorrow.'

10

Christmas Day dawned bright and clear, as Janine had every reason to know because Tamsyn was up while it was still quite dark outside. She carried her bulging stocking into her mother's bed in triumph, and together they opened it, Janine watching the delight on her daughter's face as she delved into a huge bedsock of her grandmother's, always kept safe for this particular purpose. Then it was Janine's turn to exclaim with delight as Tamsyn presented her with a parcel carefully wrapped in holly-patterned paper.

'Oh darling, how lovely,' she cried as she stripped off the paper and discovered a little vase inside.

'It is, isn't it?' agreed Tamsyn as she looked in admiration at the green plaster basket she had chosen. 'I saw it in the village and it cost 50p, so I knew you'd like it.' Janine hugged her daughter, tears springing to her eyes. 'How right you were, Tam. I love it. Thank you. I took my present for you over to Chariswood to go under the tree there for after lunch, so I'm afraid you'll have to wait until then.'

'That's all right,' said the little girl. 'Annabel and Caroline have their presents after lunch too. Anyway, I've had Gran's toboggan. That's brilliant! Do you think it will snow?'

'I don't know,' replied Janine. 'We can but hope. Gran'll be pleased you like the present. I've been keeping it hidden under my bed and I was terrified you'd discover it there!'

After breakfast they went to church in the village before preparing to drive to Chariswood for lunch. Tamsyn collected a shopping basket and in it carefully arranged the gifts she had bought for Sir Gavin and Lady Hampton, Mrs Meredith, Annabel and Caroline.

The question of presents had per-plexed Janine somewhat. She felt they could not go to spend Christmas with the Hamptons without gifts, and yet she was still faced with a dilemma; token gifts looked meagre and proper presents might look ostentatious, particularly if the Hampton family settled for the former. Her decision had been eased however, when Gavin had rung her to explain about their present for Tamsyn.

'Annabel and Caroline are being spoiled rotten by their father. As he's not here he's told Sandra to get them a pony each. Barrel's getting too small, even for Caroline. The thing is, would you allow Tamsyn to accept Barrel? She'd be able to ride him for some time yet.'

Janine was staggered by the proposal and hardly knew what to answer. She knew of course, that such a present would perfect Tamsyn's Christmas, and that the little girl would be thrilled to have the beloved Barrel for her own, but it did seem an excessive present from people so recently encountered, such new-made friends. Immediate arguments and considerations came to mind, but it appeared that Gavin had anticipated them all.

'She can continue to keep him here until the summer and then he can live out in the field below your house. My own horses are often there anyway. We'd like to think he'd gone to a good home. The tack you can have on loan, it really only fits Barrel anyhow so we shan't be needing it.'

Slightly bemused Janine had agreed to let Tamsyn accept the pony on the understanding that when she grew too big to ride him he would revert to the Chariswood stable to be sold or retired as they chose.

The Hamptons' generosity made Janine revise her own presents for Tamsyn. While the little girl was off round Churton, the nearby town, buying presents for everyone at Chariswood, Janine bought new jodhpurs and hard hat, so that Tamsyn could ride her new pony in style. She had them packed up and delivered to Chariswood so that the secret should be preserved and then hurried on to buy for Lady Hampton a beautiful azalea, Sandra, talc and soap, books on riding for the girls — all very unexciting, but safe. Gavin presented her with her greatest problem. She wanted to buy him something a little different, something to reflect her gratitude to him for his support over the past two weeks, and yet she did not want her present to be open to misinterpretation. At last she had settled for a pair of sheepskin gloves, highly unimaginative but the best she could think of in the short space of time she had to choose. She rejoined Tamsyn who had completed her own purchases and was waiting impatiently in the car.

Now, as they set out for Chariswood, Tamsyn immaculate in her red velvet party frock, all the presents were placed on the back seat; and hidden in the boot were a shirt and sweater for Tamsyn to wear with her new jodhpurs when she discovered the wonderful fact that Barrel was hers.

As they drew up in front of Chariswood, the door burst open and Caroline and Annabel rushed out to welcome them, exclaiming excitedly at the sight of the parcels in the back of the car. These were all carried indoors and disposed with a heap of others round the Christmas tree in the drawing-room. As soon as they heard the noise of the Sherwoods' arrival, Gavin, Lady Hampton and Sandra emerged from there with smiles of welcome. Annabel and Caroline carried Tamsyn off to show her what they had had in their stockings and Lady Hampton led Janine back to the fireside.

'Happy Christmas, my dear,' she said. 'We haven't given any of our main presents yet, we waited for you. We'll do it after lunch, I think.'

'Annabel and Caroline couldn't have had their presents and kept the secret from Tamsyn. They've had stockings of course, even though they don't believe in Father Christmas any more,' said Sandra.

'So I should think,' interposed their grandmother. 'One's never too old for a stocking!'

'So I noticed, Mother!' laughed Sandra. 'Anyway,' she went on, 'we've laid them a trail to follow after lunch, eventually it leads to the treasure!' As she spoke she accepted a goblet of mulled wine from her brother. 'Do try some of Gavin's concoction, Janine, it really warms you down to your toes. You are looking slim, today,' she sighed. 'I wish I had your figure,' she glanced ruefully from Janine's softly curving figure delicately displayed in a clinging jersey dress of ocean blue which picked up the elusive colour of her eyes and showed off the fair hair curling at her neck, to her own immaculately cut dress of brown silk which covered her rather dumpy person. 'However,' she declared, 'I'm not dieting today. I'm really going to enjoy my Christmas lunch.'

'Diet on Christmas Day!' exclaimed Lady Hampton. 'I should think not indeed.'

'Will you take a glass of my concoction?' Gavin asked her, 'or will you have something else?'

'Concoction, please,' answered Janine and smiled at him over the glass he handed her. The pungent smell of cinnamon and cloves assailed her nostrils and she sniffed appreciatively, beginning to feel glad they had come.

'Happy Christmas, everyone. Every happiness to you,' Gavin said, raising his glass. His greeting was to everyone, but as they raised their glasses in return, Janine's eyes met his in a look that seemed to penetrate her soul and she knew without doubt that he spoke to her alone. The moment passed unnoticed by Lady Hampton and her daughter, but Janine's heart turned over in a mixture of fear and happiness at the intensity of his look; she found her hand was shaking and she had to put her glass down so as not to spill her wine. The next time she dared to raise her eyes in Gavin's direction the moment might never have been, he was in casual conversation with his sister about one of the tenant farmers on the estate, and Janine was able to regain her self-possession and turn calmly to answer a question from Lady Hampton.

Lunch was a noisily happy affair, with Gavin presiding over a huge turkey and Lady Hampton dispensing Christmas pudding, the smallest quantity of which seemed adequate to conceal a shining new ten pence piece. And when they had eaten and drunk so much they could hardly get up from the table, Lady Hampton led them all back to the drawing-room to attack the pile of presents at the bottom of the tree. Among those presents there was a small oblong parcel for Janine, wrapped with gold paper and blue ribbon, labelled 'Happy Christmas from Gavin'. She found her hands trembled a little as she untied the ribbon and then she smiled with pleasure as the paper revealed a bottle of her favourite perfume. How had he known? She glanced up and found him watching her across the confused noise of Christmas and again she saw something in his eyes which brought unwelcome colour to her cheeks, a tenderness behind his easy smile which made her uncertain and confused. But despite the beating of her heart, she thanked him calmly enough and accepted his thanks for the gloves as well-accustomed friends might do.

'Now then, children all, come into the hall,' called Gavin, his eyes alight at their excitement. The three girls rushed into the hall and waited eagerly while the grown-ups followed at a more sedate pace.

'Now then,' said Gavin looking round at their expectant faces, 'I have something for each of you.' Retiring behind a chair, he retrieved three small blocks of wood and handed one to each girl. Attached to each block was the end

of a coloured piece of string, red for
Caroline, blue for Annabel and green
for Tamsyn. They stared at these
without comprehension and Gavin
laughed and said simply, 'Wind up the
string and see where it leads you.'

Immediately all three were winding
furiously and following their separate
strings through the downstairs rooms
and out into the garden. The heavy
louring sky which obscured the earlier
sunshine was quite unnoticed as the
girls, still winding feverishly, twisted in
and out of the trees and shrubs until at
last they headed towards the stables.
Janine followed Tamsyn who was
almost running, laughing with excitement, and she saw her daughter's face
register wondrous disbelief as she
suddenly realised where her green
string was leading her. She reached
Barrel's stable and paused at the door
to glance uncertainly back at her
mother before she followed the string
inside to its end, knotted to Barrel's
halter. A note was tied there too and

Tamsyn read 'For Tamsyn, with love from all the Hamptons'. Her cries of joy were echoed in the adjoining stables as Annabel and Caroline found their new ponies waiting patiently for them. Each child rushed to smother Gavin, Lady Hampton, Sandra and Janine in hugs and kisses, irrespective of who had given what.

'Quick ride before tea?' suggested Gavin with a twinkle and immediately the girls were flying back to the house to don their jodhpurs, Tamsyn pausing to hug her mother yet again.

'Now I see,' she cried. 'I was so pleased with my new jods before, Mummy, but it'll be just brilliant with Barrel for my very own.'

The ride led by Gavin, was a great success and was only cut short by the early onset of darkness and the flutter of a few flakes of snow. The children arrived flushed and excited to disturb the gentle slumber of their grandmother and mothers before the fire, all talking at once, all relating the events of the afternoon. They trooped noisily in to have tea, devouring cakes and sandwiches as if they had not eaten for a month rather than having disposed of an enormous Christmas lunch only three hours earlier. Tea was followed by hilarious games of charades and at last Janine said it was time for her and Tamsyn to go home.

'Can I go and say goodnight to Barrel first?' implored Tamsyn, when her cries of dismay at leaving had no effect.

'Come on then,' said Gavin. 'I'll come with you.'

Annabel and Caroline stayed indoors, but Janine, Tamsyn and Gavin braved the cold and walked round to the stables. Tamsyn threw her arms round the pony's neck and whispered, 'You're really mine now Barrell.' He nuzzled against her and blew softly down his nose.

'Uncle Gavin, you're very kind to give me Barrel,' the child remarked as they walked back through the darkness to collect their things from the house.

'I'm glad you like him,' replied Gavin.

'And I like you,' said Tamsyn. 'Uncle Gavin,' she went on, 'When you get married will the person you marry change into a lady?'

Janine was horrified by her daughter's candid question and drew breath to rebuke her, but closed her mouth without speaking as she heard Gavin replying gravely, 'Ladies don't become ladies just because they marry lords or knights, though they are then called 'Lady'. Being a lady has little to do with whom you marry, it's a natural quality, you're either a lady or you're not; being a lady is instinctive.'

Janine was glad the darkness covered her confusion at Tamsyn's question, particularly when it increased as Tamsyn considered Gavin's reply for a moment and then said, 'I see, like your mother.'

'And yours,' said Gavin.

'Come on Tam, that's enough questions for now.' Janine's voice was strangely husky as she tried to sound normal. 'We must say goodbye and thank you and go home. It's been a lovely day, hasn't it?'

They collected the other gifts they had received and retrieved Tamsyn's discarded party clothes from the heap on Caroline's bedroom floor. When everyone had gathered in the hall to say goodbye, Tamsyn hugged each of them in turn and said, 'Thank you for giving me Barrel. It's been the best Christmas I ever remember.'

Gavin alone went out with them into the cold darkness, everyone else having returned to the warmth of the drawing-room. He loaded the presents and Tamsyn into the back seat, then paused beside Janine and took her hand.

'Thank you for coming,' he said.

'Thank you for asking us, we've had a lovely day.'

The words were conventional, but as she spoke Janine felt his grip tighten on her hand and knew her fingers returned his clasp. He leaned forward and very gently brushed her lips with his; no more than a butterfly's touch, but enough to set her senses reeling at the masculinity and proximity of him. Suddenly breathless she sat down in the driver's seat of the car and he closed the door for her. Through the open window he said, 'See you soon. Come over and visit Barrel whenever you like, Tamsyn, he's yours now, remember.'

Janine drove home in a daze. It was certainly not the first time she had been kissed since Harry left her, if indeed the brief salute could be counted as a kiss; but up until now at any sign of interest in her from a man, she had instinctively withdrawn, her fear a bastion round her, and any physical advances had been firmly repelled. But when Gavin Hampton had touched her, her barriers crumbled and she found herself aching to kiss him properly. The passionate side of her nature, so long restrained and starved, had suddenly reasserted itself and she was frightened of the response she had felt at his kiss. She was glad Tamsyn had been there, an unwitting chaperone.

Tamsyn, completely unaware of her mother's inner turmoil, prattled happily about the day, her questions requiring no answers and her conversation needing no attention.

11

The next day Tamsyn was awake early and itching to go over to Chariswood to ride Barrel. Janine insisted that she waited until after lunch.

'We must give them time to themselves,' she said. 'We can't be there every minute of the day. You can write your thank you letter to Granny for your lovely toboggan this morning and we'll do things together; then after dinner you can walk over the hill to see Barrel if you promise to come home before dark.'

'That's not very long,' complained Tamsyn.

'It's long enough for today,' replied her mother. 'I don't want you taking advantage of the Hamptons' kindness.'

'Uncle Gavin said I could go whenever I liked,' muttered Tamsyn.

'But I've said you can't,' said Janine

sharply. Then she added gently, 'I don't want us to be a nuisance. You can go as often as you like within reason, but not until after lunch today.'

Recognising her mother's tone of voice, Tamsyn sighed and set about her letter to her grandmother. The toboggan was a lovely one, shiny wood with metal runners and as she gazed out across the wintry fields, brown and bare under a leaden sky, Tamsyn thought there was a good chance she would be able to try it out before many days had passed.

Immediately after lunch Janine gave way to the entreaty in her daughter's eyes and Tamsyn, arrayed in her new riding clothes, set off over the hill, scurrying along under the cold grey December sky with a promise that she would be home before dark. Janine settled down to some dressmaking, trying to concentrate her mind on what she was doing, but time and again she found her hands had fallen idle as her thoughts turned to Gavin Hampton.

Dare she follow her heart and look to him as part of her future, or should she rebuild her shattered defences and retreat to safety behind them? She felt that there was more between them than casual friendship; the link between them had grown stronger, but with the spectre of Harry's betrayal still haunting her, was she able to forget her fears and commit herself again, this time to Gavin? Here she pulled herself up short. Perhaps he did not want that sort of commitment anyway; perhaps he was looking for a far less lasting relationship, a few hours' stolen happiness with no strings. Janine considered how she would feel if this turned out to be the case, but came to no conclusion and managed, for a while at least, to push the whole thing from her mind. Maybe she had imagined too much into things anyway and he was merely being kind, as his mother was kind, but that thought brought no consolation.

The day had remained overcast and Janine had worked with the light on all afternoon, so she did not notice the darkness stealing across the hills until she stopped to make herself a cup of tea and glanced out of the window. To her amazement she saw a sprinkling of snow covering the garden and the sky heavy with more. She realised with a jolt that Tamsyn should be home. Cup of tea forgotten, she crossed to the telephone and dialled the Chariswood number and was relieved to hear Tamsyn had not started home in the snow alone.

'I'll come and fetch her,' Janine said. 'I'd rather she didn't try and walk home in this.'

'I'll bring her over if you like,' offered Gavin. 'She's having tea with the others at the moment. I'll drop her round when she's finished.'

'No, don't worry, I'm on my way.' And without giving him time to argue Janine hung up. She did not want Gavin to come to the house so that she might have to face him alone when Tamsyn had gone upstairs. Her seething thoughts had brought her no

166

conclusions; the only thing of which she was certain, was that she did not know her own mind and was determined not to be forced into any premature decisions.

Quickly Janine found her sheepskin, gloves and hat, and, locking the doors behind her, braved the swirling snow and hurried to her car. As she drove down the twisting lane to the main road, she met a Land Rover coming up, which nearly forced her into the hedge, so reluctant had the driver been to stop on the hill in such conditions. Janine cursed him and edged the car slowly back on to the road, peering anxiously through the arc of windscreen cleared by the wipers. Once on the main road the driving was easier; though the visibility was not improved, the road was clear. Even so, Janine took it very steadily, slowing almost to walking pace as she took the corner by the bridge. There were few other cars about, but by the time she turned in at Chariswood's gates, she was glad to be there and determined to waste no time in collecting Tamsyn and starting for home. The child was ready for her and clambered into the car, excited by the snow.

'Go carefully,' warned Gavin, 'and if it's too bad up your lane, leave the car at the bottom and walk.'

'We'll be all right,' said Janine calmly. 'Thank you for having Tamsyn.' With a wave they were off, edging their way down the long drive to the main road. The snow was getting heavier now and a white carpet covered the road; a wind had sprung up and the flakes no longer swirled and twirled aimlessly to the ground, but were driven against the windscreen and whipped up from the road to drift against walls and hedges. Even on full beam the headlights showed very little of the way ahead.

Tamsyn was chattering at first, but by the time they reached their lane she had lapsed into silence and was concentrating as hard as her mother on the road.

'We'll have one go at getting up the

lane,' said Janine, 'and if we don't make it we'll leave the car and walk.'

Carefully she manoeuvred the car to get a straight run at the hill and then, revving the engine, let in the clutch. The car lurched forward and with the steady pressure of her foot on the accelerator started up the hill. Determined not to let the car lose its momentum, Janine took the hill rather fast, the back wheels flinging up the snow and waltzing sideways on the corners.

'Just pray we don't meet someone coming down,' thought Janine grimly as she gripped the steering wheel, wrestling with the car as it slithered and slipped in its scramble up the lane. But luck was with them and they met no one before they struggled into the parking place in front of the cottage. The lights still burned behind the curtains in the living room and through the driving snow the cottage looked warm and welcoming.

Tamsyn ran on ahead as Janine locked the car.

'You'll need the key,' Janine called after her, but Tamsyn cried, 'It's all right, it's open.'

'Open?' Janine hurried up to the front door behind her daughter. Tamsyn met her on the step.

'Mum, what have you been doing in the living-room this afternoon?'

'Only some dressmaking, I left it all out because I was in a hurry to fetch you before the weather got too bad.'

'But the bookshelves . . . '

'What about the bookshelves?' Janine closed the front door behind her and pushed past Tamsyn into the living-room. She gasped in horror at what she saw. Her material and work box were tossed to one side, all the books from the bookshelves were strewn on the floor, their bindings bent open and their pages crushed. The cushions from the chairs were all over the floor and several appeared to have burst, their white stuffing bulging out like dirty cotton wool. The doors of the sideboard were open and the drawers had been up-ended on the carpet, their contents tipped into heaps.

For a moment Janine stood in silent horror. 'Oh God,' she whispered, and stepped into the room, unable to believe her eyes.

A stifled cry from behind her made her spin round and a cry came to her own lips as she saw two men in the hall, one holding Tamsyn firmly, with a hand over her mouth, so that all Janine could see of the child's face was her terrified eyes; and the other calmly sliding the bolts on the front door.'

'You're back earlier than we expected,' he remarked conversationally. His mouth curved into a smile but his eyes were harsh and black and remained untouched by that smile. 'We're pleased to see you, of course, because so far we haven't been able to find what we're looking for, and you could possibly save us a lot of trouble.' Before Janine could ask what they were looking for, the man holding Tamsyn gave a smothered exclamation and for a second let her go. In a flash

Tamsyn was across the room and in her mother's arms.

'Little vixen!' snarled the man. 'She bit me.' He advanced ominously and Janine pushed Tamsyn behind her, blocking the doorway with her own body to protect the child.

'Leave it, Shaw,' snapped the other man and Shaw stopped, but he glared past Janine at Tamsyn and said, 'Any more tricks like that, girl, and I'll give you a hiding you won't ever forget.' Tamsyn clung to her mother at these words and Janine put a protective arm round her.

'In there and sit down,' ordered the second man with a jerk of his head towards the living-room, and, unable to do anything else when faced by two heavy men with a tendency to violence, Janine turned back into the chaos of that room and drew Tamsyn, white-faced and afraid, down into one of the big armchairs, beside her.

The two men followed them in, the one called Shaw remaining by the door while the other one, who was obviously the boss, perched, deceptively relaxed, on the arm of the other chair.

'Now then, Mrs Sherwood. Let's get down to business. Where is Harry's notebook?'

Janine looked at him blankly. She had already guessed that these men had something to do with Harry, it was clear they were not ordinary burglars, for they had not seemed interested in the few valuables there were about the house.

'Harry's notebook?'

'Harry's notebook. Come on, don't let's play games. Probably a diary or something like. He didn't have it on him when he died, it must be here.'

For a moment the implication of what he had said did not penetrate Janine's bemused brain, and then she said slowly, 'How do you know? How do you know what was in Harry's pockets?' The man gave a short laugh and said, 'Let's just say we were given the opportunity to have a look through his things.'

Then Janine realised she and Tamsyn were locked in their own house with Harry's murderers. Instinctively her arm tightened round Tamsyn's shoulders as she felt cold fear creep through her. Harry had inadvertently led his killers to Tamsyn. Janine's innermost fears had been realised. When these men had found what they had come for, or even if they did not find it, what would become of her and Tamsyn? They would be able to identify Harry's murderers, were far too dangerous to be allowed to carry tales to the police. Surely they would never hurt an innocent child of seven; Janine glanced up at the two men and knew from the harsh set of their unemotional faces that they would. Tamsyn was no safer than she. As if to prove the point the older man shot out a hand and jerked Tamsyn roughly from the chair and held her by a handful of hair so that her head was pulled back and her terrified eyes stared up at him. She gave a frightened shriek and the man brought his hand across her cheek, slapping her into stunned silence. Janine leapt from her chair to go to the aid of her daughter but the younger man, Shaw, grabbed at her, twisting one arm up behind her and murmured softly, 'If you move again I'll break your arm.' He jerked it sharply just to show how easy it would be, making Janine give an involuntary cry of pain.

'Steady, Shaw,' said the other man easily. 'Mrs Sherwood is going to give us what we're looking for, aren't you, Mrs Sherwood? Otherwise this pretty child might have to face the rest of her life with some most disfiguring scars.' Still keeping a firm hand on Tamsyn's hair, he produced an evil-looking knife with a long thin blade. He touched the blade with his thumb and then laid the point of it on the smooth soft curves of Tamsyn's cheek. The little girl was petrified, her eyes rolling with fear. Without moving the knife the man glanced up at Janine and said conversationally, 'Now then, shall we begin?'

'What do you want to know?' croaked Janine.

'Harry was very stupid,' remarked the man. 'He thought he could doublecross us all and buy his own safety with a little notebook; a notebook in which he was foolish enough to list the names and addresses of all his contacts. Not a very important document, but we wouldn't like it to fall into the wrong hands.'

Janine was not deceived by the man's casual dismissal of the importance of the notebook; clearly Harry had already been killed because of it and she knew that the man's threats to disfigure Tamsyn's face were not idle. She racked her brain for any information she could possibly give the men which might save her daughter.

'Now, Harry came here, didn't he, after he had slipped away from the hospital so neatly. He came down here and left the book in your safe-keeping — where better than with little wifey?'

'He came, yes, but he didn't leave

anything behind. He only stayed for an hour at the most and he gave me nothing.'

'Come now, Mrs Sherwood, we can do better than that.' The voice, silky smooth, was interrupted by a scream from Tamsyn and Janine saw a thin red line appear across the child's cheek where the blade had been lightly drawn.

'Don't,' shrieked Janine, 'don't hurt Tamsyn. I'll tell you all I can, but don't harm her!'

'How sensible,' purred the man. 'Begin.'

So Janine related the events of the evening Harry had come, trying to recall as accurately as possible their conversation, their movements, their attitudes; anything that might convince these terrifying men that she was telling the truth and knew nothing about any notebook. When she had finished she lapsed into silence which remained unbroken for a moment until the man said, 'You say he mentioned arranging insurance for himself. That must have been referring to the notebook.'

'It could have been,' admitted Janine, 'but he didn't explain it to me, and I wasn't part of it.'

'Which rooms did he go into?' demanded the man.

'Only in here and the hall, oh and the kitchen to see that the back door was locked. He was very scared.'

'So he should have been. So should you be if you're not telling the truth, scared for your daughter. Pretty child.'

'I have told you the truth!' cried Janine desperately. 'Why would I hide anything? Nothing I can say can harm Harry now, it's no betrayal of him, and I wouldn't risk Tamsyn even if it were,' she added passionately, remembering her mother's words that Tamsyn's safety was Janine's prime concern.

'Well, I accept that for the moment. Sit down.' Shaw pushed Janine back into the armchair, but the second man did not release Tamsyn. Still holding her by her hair, he edged her across the room to the other deep armchair, shoved her into it and perched on the arm once more, caressing his knife with his thumb.

'Right, Shaw, it has to be here, the hall or the kitchen, assuming she's not lying. So, let's search properly. Remember, it may not be the book itself, but a note, a left luggage ticket, a key, anything. Don't miss an inch. We've got all night, no one'll be out on a night like this.'

Shaw set to his task with a will, apparently enjoying the wanton damage he was doing. When he moved ornaments he merely tossed them aside so that they crashed to the floor, books he shook upside down to be sure nothing was concealed in the pages. He took the pictures from the walls looking behind them and dropped them on the floor afterwards; he opened the grandfather clock and felt inside the case, stopping the clock in the process. He ripped open more cushions and tore back the linings and hems of the curtains. He even stuck his hand up the chimney and then continued searching the room with sooty hands, leaving black smudges on the walls and paintwork.

Janine sat and watched him with dull, dispirited eyes, part of her wanting him to find something so that the search would stop, and part of her knowing that if he did the danger to Tamsyn and herself became more immediate. If only Tamsyn were not there, Janine felt she might risk making a break for it, but even with the forlorn hope of escaping to get help, she could not consider leaving Tamsyn to the tender mercies of these savage men. Janine sat curled up in the armchair trying to plan what to do if they did find what they were after. She had no illusions as to their fate then. Perhaps she could plead with them to let Tamsyn go, a child could not harm them much. But Janine knew that after this ordeal the men's features would be etched as deeply on Tamsyn's memory as on her own.

After a while when Shaw had explored every possible hiding place in the living-room, he moved on to the kitchen. The other man remained in the living-room. He had released his hold on Tamsyn's hair and she was cowering back into the armchair, too terrified to move. Janine could hear the low moan of the wind round the house and shivered at its mournful sound, a death chant in her ears.

Bangs and crashes began to come from the kitchen as Shaw threw aside pots and pans in his search out there.

Suddenly the second man announced, 'I'm hungry. Go and cook us bacon and eggs. Don't try anything funny or the child will suffer.' He pulled Tamsyn to her feet and pushed her ahead of him towards the door. Janine got up too, and found her legs weak underneath her, but she forced herself to walk steadily to the kitchen, hoping desperately that an opportunity to save them might occur out there.

The sight that greeted her made her wonder if she would be able to produce the necessary eggs and bacon. Shaw appeared to have emptied every cupboard on to the floor, joyously shaking the contents of packets and bowls into a disgusting heap of flour, sugar, coffee, butter and jam. The second man looked round him with distaste and said, 'Try the hall now, Shaw, Mrs Sherwood is going to cook us some supper, you can finish in here later if necessary.' With a firm grip once again on Tamsyn's hair, he righted a kitchen stool and seated himself on it to watch.

12

Janine made scrambled eggs and bacon and she made enough to feed herself and Tamsyn as well. She was not in the least hungry and she had to coax Tamsyn to eat too, but something inside her insisted that they take a little food to give them strength for she knew not what. Shaw had left his turning out of the cupboard under the stairs to consume a huge plate of food, then he returned to his search while Janine, Tamsyn and their gaoler sat on the stairs and watched.

When he had finished with the cupboard he turned his attention to the hall stand. Taking the coats off the hooks one by one he searched the pockets, ripped the linings for good measure and dumped the ruined garments on the floor.

'Are you quite sure he didn't go

upstairs?' demanded the other man suddenly, bringing his knife-edge to caress the tip of Tamsyn's nose.

'Quite sure, I swear he didn't!' cried Janine in panic as the blade whispered over her daughter's skin. 'He didn't go anywhere but where I said.'

'What about when you were cooking his meal? When you were in the kitchen? Did you have the door shut?'

'I don't know. No, I don't think so. I'd have seen him go. I'd have heard him on the stairs, they squeak dreadfully, it's an old house.' The man tested the stair behind him and it squeaked satisfactorily.

At that moment there was a cry of triumph from Shaw, who had discovered a binocular case hanging concealed under an old coat of Janine's. The binoculars he had thrown aside, but he drew a piece of paper from the case and handed it across to the other man. Janine saw it had her name scrawled on it in Harry's writing. For a moment she did not understand; she had no binoculars. Then realisation dawned on her, Harry must have had his binoculars, the ones Tamsyn had seen him using on the hill, with him when he came, perhaps concealed under his raincoat, and he had left them for her to find when he was safely away. Only she had not found them for they had been hidden under a gardening jacket she seldom used, and so she had not read the letter which might have saved him.

The man unfolded the single sheet of paper and read it. Then he passed it to Janine and said, 'Do you know this man?'

She stared at the letter that Harry had written, possibly while she was cooking his food.

Dear Janine

   If you don't hear from me within the week or if anything happens to me, contact Anthony Powell, 49 Chervil Road, Hammersmith and take the sealed package he gives you to the police. He'll give it to no one but you.

Harry

'Yes, I've met him a couple of times. He was a schoolfriend of Harry's.'

'He'd recognise you?'

'Probably, possibly not. It was a long time ago.'

'How about your voice? Would he know that?'

Janine shrugged wearily. 'I don't know. I doubt it, I haven't seen him for years.'

The man tossed the letter back to Shaw. 'See if that's got a phone number. Where are your phone books?' he asked turning again to Janine.

'I haven't any London books,' she said.

'Try directory enquiry,' he ordered Shaw and moved Janine and Tamsyn back into the living-room where the telephone was. Shaw picked up the receiver and then jiggled the handset irritably several times before turning to the other man and saying, 'No dialling tone, phone's out of order.' The other man snatched the receiver and rattled the phone but with no success. He dropped the receiver back into its cradle and thought for a moment.

'Well, Mrs Sherwood, it would appear we're unable to contact the good Mr Powell tonight. You will have to go and collect your package tomorrow morning. We could collect it ourselves of course, but we wouldn't want to alarm Mr Powell so that he did anything stupid. So, it'll be a nice little trip to London for you. Of course Tamsyn'll need someone to look after her while you're away, so we'll do that for you. Not here, of course, we don't want to outstay our welcome. Find her a coat, she comes with us.' These last words were spoken sharply and jerked Janine from her daze.

'You can't take her, I won't let you!' she cried in anguish.

'You can't stop me,' he replied calmly. 'When you've done your little errand to Hammersmith come back here and wait. We'll arrange to collect the parcel and return your daughter.' He paused and added with icy precision, 'Unless of course you've done anything remarkably stupid, like informing the police or opening the package. Then naturally, she will not be returned, I shall give her to Shaw to play with, he likes little girls.' Janine jerked her eyes to Shaw in horror and saw him smiling excitedly as he held Tamsyn with one hand round her neck while the other gently smoothed her hair. She fought down the urge to launch herself at the perverted man, scratching his eyes and tearing at his face to remove that lascivious smile; but she knew that they would not hesitate to kill her if necessary now that they knew where their precious book was. Though she could make their attaining it easier, she was not indispensable and then Tamsyn would have no one. So she curbed her hatred of them both and said quietly, 'I shan't go to the police, I'll get the book and come back here. Just leave Tamsyn alone; it's got nothing to do with her.'

'Get her coat.'

'Couldn't you wait until morning, let her have a little sleep first?' begged Janine looking at Tamsyn drooping with fear and exhaustion.

'Are you expecting someone?' The man spoke sharply and strode across to the window to lift the tattered curtain.

'No, nobody, I just thought . . . '

'Christ, we must move or we'll get snowed in.' His exclamation cut through her words and Shaw, releasing Tamsyn, joined him at the window. Free suddenly, Tamsyn rushed into Janine's arms and the tears she had been holding back so bravely flowed down her face, her little body shaking with sobs.

Both men turned away from the window.

'Get that child a coat. We're leaving now or we'll be snowed in.'

'You can't have her, I won't let you

take her. You'll have to kill me first!' Janine cried in desperation, clutching Tamsyn to her.

The man answered very softly, 'We shan't kill you. It's the child we shall kill.' He paused for a moment while his words sank in and then added, 'Hurry up,' and nodded towards the heap of discarded coats in the hall. Unable to fight them any more, Janine took Tamsyn out and picked up her anorak. Shaw had ripped the lining and it hung in tatters. She moved to go upstairs to fetch Tamsyn a warmer sweater to go underneath it.

'Not upstairs,' the man barked at her and she spun round.

'That — that animal — has ruined Tamsyn's coat. She needs a thick sweater to go underneath.'

She saw Shaw's eyes blaze at her description of him, but the other man grated, 'Forget it, Shaw, and get the kid a sweater.' Shaw pushed past them and went up the stairs. Janine heard him smashing things in her bedroom and the fury rose in her at his gratuitous destruction, but still terrified for Tamsyn, she controlled her rage, regretting too, her comment about Shaw, fearing his retribution later.

'Come on, Shaw,' shouted the other man, glancing at his watch, and with lumbering tread Shaw reappeared, carrying a white Aran sweater for Tamsyn.

Janine helped her daughter into the jersey and pulled on her wellingtons, the tattered anorak and a pair of mittens. Shaw had ripped the hood away in his search, but Janine retrieved a warm woollen hat from the pile of clothes on the floor and jammed it down on Tamsyn's head. She drew her into her arms and hugged her tightly, whispering in her ear, 'Don't worry, my darling, I'll do just what they say and you'll be back with me very, very soon, I promise. Be brave, Tam darling, be brave.'

'Get the Land Rover started,' ordered the man and Shaw pulled open the front door to go outside. As he did so the wind howled in, driving a flurry of snow before it. Shaw drew back, but the second man snapped, 'Hurry or even the Land Rover won't cope.' Shaw battled his way out to where the vehicle was hidden, further up the lane, while the other man took Tamsyn in his arms and turned to Janine.

'Her safety is up to you, Mrs Sherwood. I'll keep Shaw away from her provided you play your part. When you can get out through this snow and have got the packet from Powell, come back here and wait, I'll be in touch.' Hoisting Tamsyn over his shoulder he opened the door again and disappeared into the blizzard outside.

For a moment the door stood ajar and the snow blew in frosting the floor of the hall. Janine felt numb, her feet like lead as she stared at the half-closed door. Despite the man's warning, Janine knew she could not cope with this alone; she dared not call the police for Shaw's lewd grin was far too close, and her thoughts turned to Gavin.

Suddenly she heard the roar of the Land Rover as it laboured down the lane and, galvanised into action, she slammed the front door shut and dived for the telephone, praying it was not still out of order, but the man had anticipated her and had ripped the connection from the wall. The thought of reaching Gavin dominated her mind and enabled her to press the vision, of what Tamsyn might be suffering, a little further back, so that she could plan for her daughter's deliverance without being side-tracked into the terrors Tamsyn might be facing, and her brain become numbed again. She poured herself a stiff shot of her Christmas brandy and forced herself to consider her position.

'I must get to Gavin, he'll know what to do.' She downed her brandy and went upstairs, ignoring the shambles Shaw had made of her bedroom, and with deliberate care she prepared herself to face the blizzard. She dressed in thick tights, warm trousers and sweaters and her sheepskin jacket. Over her tights she put heavy socks and drew on her wellingtons. With gloves and hat she felt able to venture out and opened the front door. The snow had drifted against the cottage wall, but she followed the tracks the men had made as they floundered to the Land Rover and reached the mound of snow that was her car, with comparative ease, but she saw at once it would have to be dug out. In feverish haste she returned to the house and went through it to collect a spade from the back porch.

It took Janine half an hour to shovel the snow away from the car and clear a track to the lane. It was difficult to see what she was doing as she had only the outside light to aid her and that was almost obscured by the falling snow. By the time she had finished she was sweating under all the warm clothes she had worn against the bitter cold, but without pausing to regain her breath she threw the spade into the back of the car and climbed into the driving seat.

The car was slow to start and Janine felt a wave of panic rising inside her as the engine coughed and spluttered and failed to catch, but at last choked into life; and with gentle pressure on the accelerator, she nursed it until, warmed through, it was running sweetly. Then with her heart in her mouth she began to back the car towards the lane. The wind had dropped a little and the snow fell more softly now; even so, the wipers struggled to clear the windscreen, and she could see nothing out of the back window. To reverse the car, Janine had to open her door and lean right out and as she inched her way along, the snow drifted into the car, covering her with a light frosting.

At last she reached the lane and began to turn the wheels to point the car down the hill; they whirred and spun and failed to find a grip. In desperation Janine got out, took the spade and dug away behind the wheels. Panting with the exertion and clammy from sweat and melted snow trickling down her neck, she cleared a patch down to the tarmac of the lane and got back into the car. The engine was still running, she had not dared to switch it off, and gradually she eased the car round so that it was headed down the hill. In the beam of the headlights she could see the tracks of the Land Rover, already filling up with snow. She glanced at her watch. It was midnight, they had left with Tamsyn nearly an hour ago. She fought down the surge of panic and concentrated on getting the car down the treacherous lane to the main road. Patches of the road were almost clear where the wind had driven the snow into the hedges, but in other places it was deep, the wheels spun furiously and the car kept moving only because it was on a hill.

Janine tried to keep in the Land Rover's tracks, but it had a broader wheel base and it was this that caused her final disaster. Following the tyre marks she gathered too much speed and with her wheels only half on the compressed snow, she hit something concealed in the softer snow of the verge. The car shuddered and the steering wheel whipped through Janine's icy fingers. The car slewed round at right angles to the hill and slid off the road ending up bonnet-first in a snow drift. Janine, jolted forwards, crashed her forehead on the steering wheel; the engine died and there was a moment's utter silence before Janine struggled free of her seat belt and tried to open the door of the car. It was difficult to force it through the snow, but she managed to open it sufficiently to squeeze out, only to flounder in the deep snow outside. Dragging herself clear she reached the comparative safety of the lane, and looked in despair at her car. The front wheels were buried in the snow drift and the angle of the rest of the car suggested that they were in the ditch which ran beside the road. Without a tow the car was immovable. Tears of bitterness coursed down

Janine's cheeks as she stared at the car, a darker shape in the darkness, balanced tipsily on its nose in the snow.

'Oh God,' she cried aloud. 'What do I do?' Her voice was smothered by the steadily falling flakes and she had never felt such despair. For a moment she was tempted to give up, to let her exhaustion overwhelm her and collapse into blissful unconsciousness in the snow, but at the vision of Tamsyn's terrified face as the man had carried her out, her determination reasserted itself.

'I must get Tamsyn back, I must get to Gavin,' and with renewed strength she turned her back on the useless car and considered what to do next. Should she walk to Chariswood, reaching the main road and following it round the hill? It was several miles and could take her all night.

'If only I had skis I could go over the top,' she thought, but she balked at the idea of floundering over the hill to Chariswood in deep snow, hampered by darkness. It would be a much shorter journey, however, than following the roads; they too might well be blocked with drifting snow, none of them was lit by street lamps so the darkness would be as difficult there as on the hilltop.

'I must get a torch, whichever way I go,' she said aloud. 'Why didn't I think of that before? How stupid to set off without one, I must have been crazy?' With this as a first priority fixed in her mind she set off up the lane to the house.

She found the flashlight and was relieved to see that the batteries were fairly strong when she tested it in the living room. As she swung it round the room over the confusion left by the two men it flashed on the steel runners of Tamsyn's toboggan, tossed carelessly behind the Christmas tree. It was as if a bell rang in Janine's head and she knew then how she was going to get to Gavin. She carried the sledge out to the front door and set it on the snow. Pulled on its rope the toboggan slid easily over the ground and Janine began to believe she could really reach help at last. She left the cottage lights on to use as a beacon to help guide her across the hill, and dragging the sledge behind her she set off up the lane, her determination to reach Gavin driving her steadily forward.

The snow had eased off a little now and as Janine gained the top of the hill where she would have to leave the lane and follow the bridle path along the ridge, the moon broke through the clouds. It was little more than a quarter full, but reflected off the snow it gave a strange, cold light which enabled Janine to recognise familiar landmarks once she had left the comparative safety of the lane.

The snow was several inches deep along the ridge, but there were few drifts as the wind had whirled the snow off the exposed hilltop and wrapped it in fantastic sculptures round the trees and bushes a little lower down. She no longer needed the torch to see her way and when she looked down over the slopes to her house nestling in a fold in the hill, she could see the lights and pinpoint her position. Still dragging the toboggan behind her, she reached the place where the bridle path cut down through the trees to the fields below, beyond which, shrouded in darkness and at present invisible to her, stood Chariswood.

The path was steep and wound between trees which shut out the moonlight, leaving only a faint luminescence from the snow. Janine set the sledge on the path and, sitting on it, eased it forward with her feet. The toboggan gathered speed and hurtled off the path into some bushes, tipping its rider unceremoniously into the snow. Cursing everything, Janine extricated herself and the toboggan from the bushes and tried again, this time keeping her heels dug into the ground as brakes to slow her descent. It took her a little while to master the steering and twice more she was deposited into the snow at the side of the path; but she was making progress and, she decided, it was still quicker than walking.

At length she left the copse behind and emerged on to the open fields above Chariswood. She could see the trees that sheltered the house now and realised with a sob of relief that her goal was in sight.

She crossed the fields ahead of her in fine style. The slopes were steep enough for the toboggan to slide easily over the snow and this time she travelled lying on her stomach with her feet trailing behind her to slow her rate of descent if necessary. Steering in the open fields was not such a problem and she covered the distance to Chariswood with tremendous speed. It was exhilarating, and had the circumstances been different, Janine would have been enjoying herself immensely. As it was, the swift descent, flying over the snow in the fitful moonlight, cleared her mind a little and when she finally came to rest in the field next to Barrel's paddock, she forgot how tired she was and picked her way round the paddock towards the stables and the house; the sledge bumping along behind her, and the wavering torchlight cutting a swathe through the darkness in front.

13

The labradors, Jason and Samson, created a tremendous din when Janine finally arrived at the front door and pounded upon it with its heavy black knocker. For a moment, only the dogs replied, but as she crashed the knocker again and again, a shaft of light pierced the darkness and played on the snow and a window above her opened from which Gavin called, 'Who's there? What's the matter?'

Janine stepped back from the door into the pool of light and looking up at the window and the dark silhouette of Gavin, she called, 'It's me, Janine. Gavin, can I come in?' Her voice cracked as she spoke. She heard him say, 'Hold on, darling, I'm coming.'

Perhaps because of his natural use of the endearment, the last of her self-control ebbed away and when he opened the door, he found her standing on the doorstep with tears streaming down her face. Without a word he gathered her into his arms and held her close for a moment before guiding her into the drawing-room where the last embers of the fire glowed in the grate. He had installed her in a chair and set about reviving the fire, when Lady Hampton came in wearing a pale-blue dressing gown and with her hair caught up in a hair net.

'Janine, my dear!' she exclaimed. 'Whatever is the matter? Gavin, I'll do that, you get the girl a drink.' Gavin left the fire to his mother and poured Janine a large brandy. Lady Hampton soon had the fire blazing again and turning to Janine she said, 'You're soaking wet and blue with cold — come on, get out of those wet things.'

Janine gulped at her brandy and said, 'I can't, not yet, Tamsyn . . . '

'Janine, where is Tamsyn?' Lady Hampton spoke sharply, realising that something must have happened to the child, but Janine responded wearily. 'I don't know, we've got to go and find her. No, we've got to go to Hammersmith.'

'Hammersmith!' Gavin exclaimed. 'Look, Janine, you'd better get your breath and explain properly, from the beginning.'

So, little by little, with several pauses to collect her thoughts, she recounted the events of the evening, while the Hamptons listened in ever-increasing horror. When she had finished, Gavin strode towards the telephone and Janine cried out, 'No, Gavin! Not the police!'

'Janine, we must. They must be told.'

'It's all right for you, she's not *your* daughter.' Janine spoke bitterly and immediately Gavin returned to her side. Kneeling down by her chair he took both her hands in his.

'Janine, listen to me. This is too dangerous for us to play around with. Tamsyn's life is at stake, I know, and so I think is yours. When you've been and collected this parcel from this Anthony Powell, what happens then? If the notebook is as important as it would appear, they aren't simply going to hand Tamsyn back when they've retrieved it, you both know too much, you can identify them and they won't be able to risk that. Remember it's almost certain that they were involved in Harry's death too. Both of you are going to endanger them. We must tell the police what has happened. They'll know how to get Tamsyn back for you. Let me phone them, please.' His eyes held hers until she had to turn away.

'Gavin's right,' said Lady Hampton quietly.

'All right,' Janine whispered, unable to combat their determination.

'And you, my dear, whatever happens after Gavin has phoned the police, must change into dry clothes before you catch your death of cold,' insisted Lady Hampton.

'I'll find her some, Mother.' Sandra spoke softly from behind Janine's chair and Janine turning, realised that Sandra must have slipped into the room while she was telling her story.

Gavin, standing by the telephone, replaced the receiver in disgust.

'Out of order,' he said. 'No dialling tone. The snow must have the lines down somewhere. Probably what affected your phone earlier, Janine.'

Janine stared wide-eyed. 'But what are we going to do? We can't get hold of the police.' Two minutes before she had been firmly against involving the police, but now when it seemed impossible to contact them, she was afraid every passing moment would make it too late.

'Don't worry,' said Gavin. 'We'll go to them.'

'But the snow . . . '

'We'll get there,' he reassured her. 'I promise. You go with Sandra and put on some dry clothes while I go and get dressed too.'

Janine looked at him in surprise and noticed for the first time that he was clad only in pyjamas, dressing gown and slippers.

'Off you go,' he urged, gently pushing her towards the door.

It was only a matter of minutes later that Janine returned downstairs wearing Sandra's clothes from the skin out, to find Gavin shrugging himself into his sheepskin coat.

'We'll take the tractor from the farm,' he announced as he looked up and saw her on the stairs. 'Warmer?'

Janine managed a weak smile and nodded.

'Good girl. Let's go then.' He turned to Lady Hampton who stood in the drawing-room doorway, anxiety lining her face.

'Don't worry, Mother. We'll get through in the tractor.' Lady Hampton nodded and then crossed the hall to where Janine stood, pale and determined. Giving her a quick hug, Lady Hampton said, 'I know it's a silly thing to say really, but try not to worry, the police'll get her back.'

Gavin swung the front door open and they stepped out into the night. Taking Janine's arm, he led her round the house to the farm buildings beyond, lighting their way with a powerful flashlight. The snow had begun to fall again, drifting thickly down to lay another layer of white powder on the freezing crust of the earlier snow; the trees sheltering the house bent under the burden, their branches undisturbed as the wind still slept.

They reached the tractor shed with comparative ease, though Gavin never loosened his hold on Janine's arm to steady her if necessary. Once inside, he switched on the light and Janine saw a huge tractor with an enclosed cab standing silently waiting. The tread on the enormous wheels stood out in ridges and looked comfortingly efficient giving Janine a spark of hope that they might indeed get through.

'Climb up inside,' called Gavin, collecting a spade from the back of the shed and putting it into the cab. Janine did as she was told and waited while Gavin threw open both shed doors; he climbed up beside her and said, 'Off we go then, keep your fingers crossed.'

The engine leapt to life at first touch and with the powerful beam of the head-lights carving a path of brilliance through the night, they edged out into the yard. For a moment Janine thought the trac-tor wheels were going to spin as her car wheels had, but the immense tread of the tyres bit truly through the snow to grip the ground beneath.

Keeping to a crawl, Gavin eased the tractor out of the yard and along the track that led first to the drive and on to the main road. The wipers worked double time to keep the windscreen clear and both Gavin and Janine peered intently through the cleared space as they churned their way through the snow under an arch of snow-laden trees. Small drifts had built up across the drive, but keeping to its steady pace, the tractor carved its way through them and before very long they had reached Chariswood's gates and emerged on to the snow-covered main road. Gavin turned the tractor towards the village and they maintained their progress until they reached the corner by the bridge across the river.

Suddenly Janine cried out, 'Stop! Oh stop!'

'What's the matter?' asked Gavin, slowing the tractor to a halt and peering out of the side window. 'What've you seen?'

'The Land Rover, or a Land Rover anyway. It's crashed by the bridge.' She made a move to climb out of the cab, but Gavin stayed her and said quietly, 'Hang on a minute, let's get some light on the scene.' He started the tractor again and manoeuvred it round so that its headlamps illuminated the crashed Land Rover, then they both scrambled down and struggled through the snow towards it. Janine looked fearfully inside, terrified of what she might find; her heart pounding at the thought of Tamsyn injured, freezing inside the

212

wreck. But it was empty. The car had spun off the road, travelling away from the cottage, but apart from that there was no other indication that it was even the same one in which the kidnappers had escaped; she had no idea of its number or even its colour.

'There's nothing here,' said Gavin gently when he had looked in, round and under the crashed vehicle. 'If it was them, they got out. See if you can see where their footprints go.' But it was difficult to tell, for Janine and Gavin had disturbed the snow immediately round the wreck and the steadily falling flakes had smoothed the tell-tale prints leading away into the darkness.

'Come on,' said Gavin. 'Let's go on to the police. It's still the best thing we can do.'

The Friars Bridge police station was little more than an office tacked on to the police house, which stood not far from the school. A panda car stood buried in a snowdrift in the drive outside and the house was in darkness, hardly surprising at nearly three o'clock in the morning.

Once again they climbed down from the tractor's cab and trudged through the snow up to the front door. Gavin rang the bell several times and then an upstairs light came on followed by the hall light, shining through the glass panels of the door and printing gleaming patterns on the snow outside.

When the door opened, a tousle-headed Constable Barnes peered at them and then, recognising Sir Gavin Hampton on his doorstep, ushered them inside.

In the police office, warmed by a powerful fan-heater, Janine told her story again while the policeman listened intently, doodling with a pencil on a pad in front of him. When she had finished he considered in silence what she had told him, only the hum of the fan-heater breaking that silence.

'It's too big for me,' he said at last. 'We must get in touch with this Sergeant Harrington. Do you still have the number he gave you?'

Janine shook her head, 'No, I don't think so. I threw it away. I didn't think I'd need it.'

'Never mind,' said PC Barnes reassuringly. 'We'll find him. And,' he added, 'he'll find your daughter, I'm certain.'

'We'll leave it in your hands, Constable,' said Gavin. 'I'm going to take Mrs Sherwood back to Chariswood now and make sure she gets some sleep. You can contact us later, as soon as you have some news.' Janine began to protest that she could not possibly sleep with Tamsyn still in danger, but Gavin cut her short.

'Of course you must sleep, we'll give you something to be sure you do. There's nothing more we can do until we're in touch with Sergeant Harrington. Constable Barnes will let us know. Nobody can move very easily in this snow, all the local police will be alerted to look for them, but I expect they've gone to ground somewhere quite close, to wait until you've done your trip to Hammersmith. If that Land Rover was theirs they won't have got very far.'

Constable Barnes reinforced Gavin's arguments and at last Janine allowed herself to be persuaded back into the tractor and returned to Chariswood.

Lady Hampton was waiting for them as they staggered into the house, cold and exhausted, and within minutes Janine was undressed and tucked into a warm bed in a spare room, a hot water bottle at her feet and another clasped in her arms. Obediently she drank the hot milk and swallowed the tablets which Lady Hampton gave her, and despite the turmoil of her mind, she sank into a deep and dreamless sleep.

When she awoke she lay for one glorious moment warm, dozing, un-remembering; then the horror of the night flooded back to her and she looked at her watch. It was twelve o'clock! She leapt out of bed, padded across the room in her borrowed nightdress and threw back the curtains to be greeted by a white and silent world. The window looked out from the front of the house and down the drive she could see the deep tracks left by the tractor; then even as she looked she saw a Range Rover crawling up the drive from the main road. At once she drew back from the window and hurriedly pulled on the clothes hanging over a chair. They were her own, dried and ready for her and she felt a burst of gratitude at the thoughtfulness of Lady Hampton and her daughter.

On her way downstairs she met Gavin coming up.

'Hallo,' he said smiling. 'I was just coming to see if you were awake. Sergeant Harrington and a super-intendent have just arrived. They're in the library.' He led the way, pausing only to ask Mrs Deeben to bring in some coffee for them all.

They spent the next hour discussing the situation and eventually conceived a plan to rescue Tamsyn from her kidnappers, while protecting both Janine and Tamsyn as far as possible.

'We've already checked at the railway station,' said Harrington. 'The line's now clear, but no one answering the description of Tamsyn and her captors got on to the morning train. I understand from Constable Barnes that a Land Rover is missing from one of the farms on the other side of the village, it's quite possible that they took that. Anyway, the next step is for you to go to London and see Powell and in the meantime we'll have your telephone repaired.'

The superintendent took her hand as he rose to go.

'Don't worry, Mrs Sherwood, we'll do our utmost to get Tamsyn back for you. We'll do exactly as we've planned and keep a very low profile, but never forget we'll be watching your every move so that you won't ever be alone, and the moment you are re-united with your daughter we'll keep you both under the closest protection. These men must not go free and they will not if we all play our part.' Janine nodded, but fear lined her face. She knew she had a counter to bargain with in the notebook and was determined not to part with it until Tamsyn was safe, but how long would they remain safe? It was a question Janine had to rely on the police to answer and, despite their assurances, still she was afraid.

14

As soon as the two policemen had disappeared down the drive in their Range Rover, Janine began to prepare for her part in the plan. She went over what she must do, with Gavin, as she forced down a meal to give her much-needed strength.

'And remember, don't take taxis,' he impressed upon her, 'you never know who's driving.' She promised to remember that and everything else and was on edge to leave. Quickly she dressed in her outdoor things again and having said goodbye to Lady Hampton and Sandra, she and Gavin set off once more in the tractor.

The snow had stopped and a pale winter sun fingered its way through the clouds, striking white fire from the snow-covered trees and glinting sharply on the windows of the house. Having gained the main road they turned towards Friars Bridge and were able to keep up a steady pace round the hill. A snow-plough and gritting lorry had already passed that way and the dark grit gave an easier grip on the partially cleared road. Before long they were at the end of Janine's lane and here they drew the tractor clear of the road so that they could walk up and look at her car. Gavin helped Janine down from the tractor and they struggled up the hill where the snow, uncleared, lay unevenly deep. Despite the sun there was no warmth in the air and their breath clouded out in front of them as they stood viewing the car still slumped into the ditch.

Gavin had a rope over his shoulder and he crouched down in the snow to attach it to the tow-hook on the back of Janine's car.

'Don't worry, Mrs Sherwood, we'll soon have her pulled out.' He spoke clearly, addressing Janine as if they were no more than acquaintances, a neigh-bour coming to the aid of another.

Janine, very much aware that they could well be under surveillance and within earshot of the watcher, forced herself to sound as calm as possible.

'This really is most kind of you, Sir Gavin, I particularly wanted to get the car out today.'

Together they uncoiled the rope and then Gavin drove the tractor into the mouth of the lane and took it steadily up the hill until he was above the stranded car. Once they had the tractor securely attached to the other end of the tow-rope, Gavin clambered back into the cab and took up the strain. Standing well clear, Janine watched anxiously as the steady pull of the tractor gradually hauled her car from the depths of its snowdrift, out of the ditch and on to the road again. As soon as it was clear, Janine darted forward, opened the door and jerked on the hand-brake while Gavin left the tractor ticking over and untied the tow-rope.

'There you are, Mrs Sherwood,' he said amiably. 'Would you like me to take it down on to the main road? We don't want you back in the ditch again, do we?' His rather patronising tone made Janine glance up at him angrily, but catching the ghost of a twinkle in his eye she said demurely, 'Thank you, Sir Gavin. Perhaps it would be best.'

He drove the car down the last few yards to the main road and turned out towards the village. Janine stumped down after him, actually quite glad she had not had to negotiate the lane herself. She found Gavin waiting for her with the engine running and still conscious of possible eyes observing them, she thanked him again and slid into the driver's seat.

'Take it steady now,' he advised, 'it's still not easy driving.' Then in a lower tone he murmured, 'Don't worry, I'll be close behind you all the while. Be brave, we'll get her back.' And banging a salute on the roof of the car with the flat of his hand, Gavin sent Janine off on the next part of her journey.

With the road newly gritted, it was

comparatively easy driving and she reached the railway station without mishap. It had been decided she should take the train because of the weather and because it would make keeping her safely observed much easier for the police. Few trains stopped at Friars Bridge, but there was one at 3.30, a slow, stopping train which reached London in the early evening. Janine left her car in the station yard and bought her ticket. It was bitterly cold on the platform and she went into the waiting room for the half-hour before the train was due. A woman with a little girl and a lone man were already waiting and they all huddled round a tiny paraffin stove making the most of its meagre heat.

At last the train drew in and Janine followed her companions out to the platform and on to the train. She chose a carriage with people already in it, feeling the need of others and when she was settled in a window seat, she let her eyes range out on to the platform in the hope of seeing Gavin there, but the platform was empty. She glanced round the carriage. Were any of the superintendent's men there? Or the kidnappers'? There was no way to tell.

The journey was long and tedious, but at last the train pulled into Waterloo. The carriage had filled up gradually as people came to London for an evening at the theatre or a night on the town. With a jolt Janine realised it was only two days after Christmas and most of these people were still celebrating. Christmas to her seemed a lifetime ago, and she swallowed hard at the recollection of Tamsyn's face as she had seen Barrel waiting for her.

The cheerful bustle as everyone poured off the train carried Janine along and she was entirely unable to tell if she was being followed or not. However she remembered the police superintendent's promise and followed his instructions; pausing only to buy an A to Z at the bookstall, she went down the subway to the underground and took a ticket to Hammersmith. Minutes later she was clattering across London in a rush-hour tube train, crushed between a large West Indian in a trilby hat and two women carrying huge parcels, who continued their conversation across Janine's face.

Who was following to protect her in such a crush? Who was following her whom she had cause to fear? She shivered in the sweaty heat of the underground, but commonsense came to her aid and she realised no one was going to harm her before she had the package in her possession; until then she would be safe enough. It was after she had collected it that she could be in danger.

Janine changed to the District Line and as she waited for the Hammersmith train she glanced casually round hoping to see some sign of her police support, but no one on the platform showed the remotest interest in her and she was wondering fearfully if they had lost her in the crush when the train came in and she surged into an already crowded carriage with another wave of determined passengers.

When she arrived at Hammersmith station she paused on the platform to consult her A-to-Z on where Chervil Road was, and having ascertained the direction she emerged into the false brightness of Hammersmith Broadway.

There had been far less snow here, and, though there was still a light covering on the roofs of the shops, where the traffic thundered round it had turned to slush and melted away, leaving dark gleaming streets and muddy pavements.

Janine set off towards Chervil Road, consulting her guide occasionally under street lamps. Away from the hubbub of the Broadway, the streets were strangely quiet and the sound of her footsteps was a muffled crunch as she passed before the blank faces of the terraced houses. The curtains were all drawn against the cold winter night and only chinks of escaping light cut through the darkness to reflect upon the dirty snow. Street lamps stood far apart creating pools of light and deeper shadows in the encroaching dark. Janine saw no one and her heart seemed to pound as loudly as her feet on the pavement.

At last she stood on the corner of Chervil Road. It differed very little from the other streets, much of it was in shadow and parked cars lined it, many of them still snow-covered. As she walked slowly peering at the houses to discover their numbers, she passed a parked car that seemed familiar, the number leapt out at her and a surge of joy went through her as she recognised it as Gavin's. It took all the determination she had not to stop, nor give the car more than a passing glance, but it gave her courage an incredible boost to realise Gavin was so close to her, watching for her safety. Obviously he had not travelled in the train for fear of being recognised as the man who had helped pull her car free, but he was here now, at the most dangerous part of her mission, ready to whip her away to safety if she were threatened as she emerged from Anthony Powell's flat.

Three houses further on she came to the one she sought, number 49. It was no different from its neighbours, with three steps up to the front door and others leading down to an area below, protected from the street by spiked iron railings. Beside the front door was a row of bells each with a name against it. Anthony Powell's was the top bell. Janine pressed it and waited. A disembodied voice said lazily, 'Yes?' and realising suddenly that there was an entryphone speaker, Janine said huskily, 'It's Janine Sherwood, Harry Sherwood's wife.'

'Janine?'

'Harry Sherwood's wife. Can I come in?'

'Top floor. Come on up.'

There was a buzz and a click and the front door opened. Janine went inside, closing the door behind her.

Anthony Powell was waiting for her

on his landing, and took her into his flat. She had only met him once or twice, soon after she and Harry were married, and remembered him as a small man with mousey hair and a moustache. So he appeared now, though he was taller than she recalled and his hair had thinned on top. He looked at her speculatively as if reassuring himself that she was the Janine Sherwood he had met before. Then seeing her pale-faced exhaustion he said, 'You look as if you could do with a drink.' He pushed her gently into a chair and crossed to a drinks trolley where he splashed a generous measure of whisky into a glass.

'Sorry I've only got whisky,' he said as he handed it to her.

'That's all right,' answered Janine. 'Thanks,' and she took a pull at the drink; the neat spirit made her splutter a little, but she felt its warmth creep down inside her and drank again.

'Well now, to what do I owe this pleasure?' Anthony Powell spoke easily but his darting eyes were sharp and penetrating. 'Where is dear Harry?'

'Harry's dead.' Janine was so tired and tense that her reply was more abrupt than she had intended, but Anthony Powell did not seem unduly surprised.

'I see.'

'He told me to come to you if anything happened to him.'

'Did anything 'happen' to him?'

'He was murdered.'

'Do we know by whom?' Powell's questions seemed almost casual, without interest, but Janine was aware of his probing eyes and knew he was sounding her out. She was determined to say nothing which might prejudice Tamsyn's release so she replied firmly, 'No.'

'I see,' said Powell again. 'How can I help you?'

'Harry said he had left a package with you to give me if I came to ask for it.'

'Did he now?'

'Yes, he did.' Janine's voice sharpened

with anxiety. 'Didn't he leave it with you?'

'He did. But should I give it to you? How do I know he's dead?'

'You don't,' replied Janine dully, 'but I need that package.'

'Wait here a moment.' Anthony Powell left the room and returned almost at once with a small parcel wrapped in brown paper and string. The knots of the string were sealed with red sealing wax and when he handed it to her, Janine saw that it was addressed to her in Harry's writing. She almost broke down at the sight of it; clutching it close to her she whispered, 'Thank God. Thank God.'

'Now, can you tell me what all this is about?' Anthony Powell spoke gently, looking down at her in the chair.

'No, I can't. Not now, perhaps not ever. Just let me take the parcel and I'll go.'

'Aren't you going to open it?' Anthony Powell was still asking his questions casually, but it was clear he was intrigued.

'No, not now. I must go.' She finished her drink in one swallow, grateful for the fire it brought. But Anthony Powell was not so easily put off.

'What was Harry mixed up in?' he asked.

'Mixed up in? I don't know what you mean.'

'Come on Janine, he must have been mixed up in something to necessitate all this cloak-and-dagger stuff; and bring that haunted look to your eyes.'

Again Janine was aware of his eyes probing her face to reach her mind but she turned away and rose from her seat with weary determination.

'I'm sorry, Anthony, if I could tell you more I would, but too much depends on my silence.' She crossed to the door and he followed her.

'If it's really that dangerous I'd better see you back to the tube,' he suggested as she stowed the vital package away in an inside pocket of her coat.

'No, thank you. It's better that I go

233

alone. I don't want to be seen with anyone.'

Anthony Powell nodded and said, 'Remember what Sherlock Holmes said, I think it was Sherlock Holmes anyway or someone like him, 'Never take the first cab that offers, nor the second.''

Janine managed a faint smile and said, 'Don't worry, I shan't take a cab at all.'

When she emerged into the street she glanced along its deserted length and then set off back the way she had come. As she reached Gavin's car, still parked at the roadside, she longed to look inside to see if he was there, but, determined not to draw the attention of unseen eyes, she turned her collar up and hurried past looking neither to right nor left of her. As she reached the corner of the street, a courting couple who had been tightly in each other's arms, came out of the deeper shadows of a doorway and drifted along the street behind her. They had their arms draped round each other's neck and paused occasionally to exchange kisses, but apart from them no one else walked the street; and when they reached the Broadway, still not far behind Janine, two punk rockers elegantly attired in denim jeans and green hair, shuffled out of a coffee-bar and followed her down the subway while the courting couple wandered into a pub for some bright lights and juke-box music.

Janine was afraid now that she had the precious package on her. Suppose someone attacked her and stole it; she would never see Tamsyn again. She stood on the platform and waited for an underground, leaning against the curved wall so that no one could approach her from behind, and searching the faces of the other passengers. The superintendent had promised her she would not be alone, but in the impersonal light of Hammersmith station, she had never felt more alone in her life. Which of the other travellers, if any, were her protection?

Which her danger?

The train drew in and she got into a carriage. The two green-haired punks got in at the other end, laughing and sharing a cigarette, and when an elderly woman pointed out they were in a non-smoker, one leered at her and said, 'So what darlin'?'

Two stations later the punks got out and a big West Indian got in and stayed in the carriage until Janine changed trains. As she found the platform for the Northern line, two young women discussing the various merits of their favourite pop groups fell in behind her and when she boarded the train for Friars Bridge, she shared her compartment with two naval ratings and a bespectacled Indian. The Indian got out at Friars Bridge as well and engaged the one and only taxi in the station yard, which followed Janine at a discreet distance. Thus it was, that unbeknown to her, the superintendent fulfilled his promise and Janine was never left unattended from the moment she left Anthony Powell's flat until the moment she parked her car outside the cottage and opened her own front door.

15

The house was in darkness and, immediately fearful as she recalled how the men had been waiting for her before, she switched on the light, then she closed the door behind her and put across both bolt and chain. Turning to the living-room, she opened its door only to pause, amazed at what she saw. She had expected to find it as she had left it the previous night; but the shambles had gone and the room was polished and glowing, with firelight jumping in the darkness and the curtains pulled against the cold night outside. Suddenly she realised she had been able to drive up the hill and that her parking space was clear of snow. She dropped her handbag on the chair and pressing her hands to her face, a sob escaped her. She switched on the table lamp and moved to the fire to warm her hands, and then she saw him, fast asleep in an armchair, the back of which had shielded him from her immediate sight. With his face relaxed in sleep Gavin looked younger, the anxious lines she had seen so recently were smoothed away and she knew at once who it was who had arranged to have her house set to rights and her drive cleared. Softly she crossed to the chair and looked down at him, a sudden longing to take his hands in hers and slip into his arms, laying her head on his chest, almost overwhelming her. She stood watching him for a moment, tears bright in her eyes and he, as if her gaze had penetrated his sleep, awoke and passing a hand across his brow saw her and jerked fully awake.

'Janine. You're back.' He jumped up guiltily. 'I meant to have a meal ready for you. I didn't put the lights on in case the house is being watched and I must have fallen asleep.' He looked down at her pale drawn face and said,

'Did you get it?'

Janine nodded wearily, and said softly, 'Thank you for being there.' He looked surprised. 'You saw the car?' She sank into the other armchair and looked at him across the hearth.

'Yes, I saw the car.'

'You gave no sign.'

'No, I was afraid I was being watched, but it encouraged me to know I wasn't alone.'

'You're a very courageous person, Janine. Keep your courage high and we'll see this nightmare through.'

'Suppose they come here and just take the parcel? It's Harry's notebook I'm sure; that's what they're looking for.'

'Listen,' said Gavin. 'In spite of their threats about Tamsyn, the kidnappers must know there's a possibility you have contacted the police and are under their protection. I don't honestly think they'll come anywhere near you except on ground of their own choosing, having planned carefully how to regain the notebook and make good their escape. Coming here, they might well be walking into a trap. But if they do,' Gavin went on grimly, 'we'll be ready for them.'

'We?'

'You don't think I'm going to leave you alone here while we wait to discover what they are going to do next, do you?'

Janine sighed. 'I hadn't really thought about it.'

'Well I have. They don't know I'm here even if they are keeping watch. I came over the hill after dark and let myself in with the estate office key. I didn't put any lights on. We'll just sit it out and wait for them to contact us. The phone's been repaired by the way. The police got a priority put on it and the engineers fixed it this afternoon. They've put a tap on it as well. Now, shall we eat?'

'Who cleared up here?'

'Mother, Sandra and Mrs Deeben. And Ned cleared and gritted the hill.

Janine, what's the matter? Don't cry!'
He gazed down at her in alarm and for
a moment Janine thought he was going
to gather her up in his arms, but as if
mastering the impulse he said firmly,
'You must eat something and then get
some sleep. Come on, let's see what's in
the kitchen, I brought a basket from
Chariswood.'

Within half an hour Janine had
drunk some soup, eaten some toast
and was asleep in her own bed; dead
to the world, thanks to the sleeping
pills Lady Hampton had sent. Her
sleep was deep and dreamless and
while she slept, free from fear for a
few hours, Gavin paced the living-
room downstairs wondering how an
exchange could be arranged to
guarantee the safety of Tamsyn. At
last, unable to think of any workable
plan, he fell into an uneasy sleep in
the big armchair before the dying fire.

In the morning Janine appeared, still
very pale, but rested, and she cooked
breakfast for them both while Gavin

kept watch on the lane from an upstairs window, carefully concealed by the curtain. He was determined they should not be taken unawares. He knew the police were watching the approaches too, but they could not come close enough without betraying their presence.

Thus they waited for two more days; each trying to conceal his mounting fear from the other; Gavin keeping watch in case an attempt was made to take the package by force, and Janine sitting with him, afraid of her own thoughts when she was alone. Each day they made a brief telephone call to Chariswood where Sergeant Harrington had his headquarters; but there was no sign of anyone and the waiting drained them all.

The second evening Janine was nearly crazy with worry. They were sitting downstairs by the fire, the windows closely curtained and the doors locked and barred against unheralded intrusion.

'Why don't they phone?' she cried suddenly, pounding her clenched fists into the cushions of her chair. 'I'm going mad! Why don't they phone?'

As she gave way to her terrified grief Gavin could hold himself from her no longer. He pulled her into his arms and rocked her gently, smoothing her curls with tenderness and soothing her pain with gentle words.

'Janine, darling, darling heart. I'm here, don't cry. It'll be all right, I promise. We'll get her back. They're working on your fear. Don't let them break you, darling. Don't let them win. Look at me, Janine, look at me and trust me.'

She raised her brimming eyes to his and saw a look there that even in her time of terror, stirred her to her innermost soul, and with another sob she flung her arms round his neck and buried her face in his shoulder.

The shrill of the telephone made them leap apart, but Gavin kept a firm hold on one of Janine's hands as she picked up the receiver with the other.

'Hallo,' she whispered. 'Janine Sherwood speaking.'

'Ah, Mrs Sherwood,' drawled a voice. 'Do you know who this is?'

'Yes, I know.'

'Good. Well now, your daughter's quite well,' he paused, 'so far. Have you got the package?'

'Yes, I've got it.'

'Very good. I trust you haven't opened it?'

'No.'

'Very sensible, remember Tamsyn's innocence depends on that. Poor Shaw, he's very frustrated just now.'

'I haven't opened it, I swear I haven't. I promise I won't.' Janine's voice rose in terror at the recollection of Shaw's cruel face, threatening Tamsyn.

'Then listen,' the voice altered from a caressing drawl to a sharp command. 'Get your car and go alone to the Herewood Service Area on the motor-way. Park the car in the far corner of the eastbound car park, leave it unlocked and wait in the lobby of the caféteria. I'll phone you there. Be there by seven o'clock tomorrow morning. Bring the package. Don't be late. Speak to no one. Remember, Tamsyn's relying on you. If you bring the police you'll never see her again.'

'Is she safe? How do I know she's safe?' Janine cried.

'You'll have to take my word for it. Don't be late.'

With a click the line went dead and Janine sunk limply back into a chair. Gavin took the receiver from her hand and replaced it; then he asked 'What did he say?'

Janine told him.

'I wonder if Harrington got a fix on where the call came from,' said Gavin. Janine had forgotten that the police had a tap on her line and she looked up at Gavin in alarm.

'They won't do anything, will they? Nothing to endanger Tamsyn?' Her voice was sharp with fear. Gavin knelt down beside her and took both her hands in his.

'They won't. Tamsyn is their first concern and they'll do everything possible to get her safely back. We'll ring them now.' As he reached for the receiver however, the telephone rang again and this time Sergeant Harrington spoke.

'We got all that, but it wasn't long enough to trace the call, but we've got enough to go on. Now, Mrs Sherwood should keep the rendezvous as arranged and when her daughter is safely back with her, we'll pick them up.'

Janine snatched the phone from Gavin and cried, 'You're not to be at that service area when I go. Any sign of a police car and they'll not bring her. Promise me you won't be there.'

'Don't worry, Mrs Sherwood, there'll be no sign of us.'

'They'll be watching for anyone looking like police. Please stay away. Surely Tamsyn is more important than this stupid notebook!'

'Of course. We shan't be in evidence. We'll even keep the traffic police away. Don't worry.'

Gavin spoke to the policeman again and then replaced the receiver.

'Now you must sleep,' he said to Janine. 'It'll take two hours to Herewood Services and so you've got an early start. Supper, then bed.'

Janine, unresisting, agreed and at last slept before the final phase of her ordeal.

It was still dark when she set off the next morning. The air was bitterly cold and the snow still covered the countryside though the main roads were clear. There was very little traffic about and Janine reached the motorway interchange in less than half an hour, and then settled down to the monotonous drive to the Herewood Service area. On the motorway there was more traffic, but nothing to bother her and for a while her mind ranged over the events of the days since Boxing Day, but she had to pull it away as she felt the tension and fear mounting. She needed to keep calm and cool to save her daughter, for she was certain it would not be as easy as it sounded. Would they ever let her and Tamsyn go free, able to recognise Shaw and the other man?

'Be brave!' Gavin had said as Janine left the house, 'I'll be waiting for you both,' and he had held her tightly for a moment in the darkened hallway as if to infuse her with extra courage from his own strength, before she set out to face the dangers awaiting her alone.

It was just after half-past six when Janine pulled in to the Herewood Service area and parked the car in the furthest corner from the facility buildings. She left it unlocked, as instructed, and crossed over to the neon-lit restaurant. It was still dark, but there were lights in the car park and she could just see the back window of her car from the window in the lobby outside the caféteria. The lobby was brightly lit. Four telephones sheltered by metal hoods were ranged along one wall and there were two padded benches beneath the window. Despite the early hour the caféteria was quite busy and people were playing the space invaders and gambling machines in the lobby, so that there was a continual clatter from machines, china and cutlery. Yet it did not penetrate her consciousness and Janine perched, rigid, on the edge of one of the benches and waited for the phone to ring. The hands moved round on a large wall clock above the phones; each minute the long hand jumped to its next appointed place and Janine found herself counting out the seconds between each jerk. At last it jumped to exactly seven o'clock. Janine turned her eyes to the telephones and knew a moment of panic as she saw they were all in use. No one could ring in because they were all engaged. The minute-hand of the clock jumped five more times before one of them became free and Janine sat there waiting, her eyes studying the patterns of the floor tiles, but her mind shrieking, 'Get off the phone!'

A woman in the end booth replaced the receiver and within seconds the phone shrilled out. Janine leapt to her feet and snatched the receiver from its cradle.

'Hallo,' she said breathlessly.

'Mrs Sherwood?'

'Yes.'

'Are you alone?'

'Yes.'

'I do hope so.' The voice was cold and sinister, not one she had heard before.

'I am. I'm quite alone. I've got what you want.'

'Good. Place the package behind the phone books in your booth. We'll collect it.'

'What about Tamsyn?' Janine asked shakily.

'Look out of the window. We're putting her in your car.' Janine turned to stare out of the window and saw in the creeping light of early day, a man walking with a fair-haired little girl to where Janine had parked her car.

'Leave the package,' instructed the voice, 'and go into the caféteria. You can watch the car from there and see your child is not removed, unless of course the contents of the package are not satisfactory. If you attempt to leave the caféteria in less than half an hour, or if you speak to anyone, your daughter will not be in the car by the time you reach it. Tamsyn will be asleep when you get to her so that she doesn't try to come and find you. All you have to do is to sit and drink a cup of coffee for half an hour, relax, and then your daughter will be waiting for you to take her home.' The tone of the voice changed as it added, 'Don't do anything stupid, Mrs Sherwood, or she won't be there. We shall be watching you. If you're sensible and keep your mouth shut, you won't hear from us again.' With a click of finality the line went dead. For a moment Janine stood as if transfixed, then she pulled out one of the phone books as if to look up a number and as she returned it to its cubby-hole under the phone, she slipped the package in behind it. Then, without taking her eyes off the back of her car where she had seen Tamsyn installed, she went into the caféteria where she could still see the car from the window, but could no longer see the telephones outside in the lobby. Glancing at her watch she saw it was seven minutes past seven; at seven thirty-seven she could leave the caféteria, not a moment before, and run to Tamsyn, asleep in the car. Why would she be asleep? She must have been drugged. Tamsyn had still been walking when Janine had seen her approaching the car, though supported a little by the man with her.

'Please God, let her be all right,' prayed Janine. 'Please, God, let her just be asleep.'

Janine took a quick glance around the cafétaria, now half full with people eating breakfast. Who was watching her to see she did not leave too soon? Nobody seemed interested in her and she recognised no one. Or did she? Suddenly her heart leapt as she realised one of the men seated at a table in a far corner eating toast and marmalade and almost hidden behind a paper was Gavin. She turned away abruptly to keep up her watch on her car. Nobody had been near it since the man had left Tamsyn in the back. She allowed herself another quick look at Gavin solemnly eating his toast. As if he felt her eyes he glanced up as he re-folded his paper, but there was no recognition in his eyes and Janine returned once again to the surveillance of her car.

'Please God, don't let his being here spoil it,' she thought, but even as the thought entered her head it was outweighed by her relief at not being alone any more.

The seconds ticked by slowly. There was a similar clock to the one in the lobby, on the restaurant wall and Janine again started counting the seconds between each jump of the minute hand, her eyes continually flicking from car to clock and back to car again. As the hands approached seven thirty-seven Janine drew a deep breath and got ready to move, but she did not actually stand up until seven-forty. There must be no mistakes in her timing.

The time from when she left the caféteria until she had the car in view again must be minimised. They must have no time to remove Tamsyn again without her knowing. As she crossed to the exit, still watching the window, she saw from the corner of her eye, Gavin folding his paper casually and standing up too.

The moment she lost sight of the car from the window, Janine ran. She hurtled through the swing doors into the lobby, out round the corner of the building and then dodging through the parked cars, sprinted across the car park to where her car stood on the far side. She flung open the back door and saw Tamsyn, breathing steadily if heavily, lying fast asleep on the back seat; and finally, succumbing to the sudden release of tension and relief, Janine burst into tears.

16

Janine heard the sound of footsteps behind her and spun round, terrified that the kidnappers had returned, but it was Gavin, approaching casually as if with no interest in Janine or her car.

'Gavin!' she cried, 'Gavin, it's all right, she's safe.'

Gavin darted to Janine's side, all caution gone for a moment, and gathered her into his arms, kissing her tears away, as he too was consumed with relief.

'My brave darling, well done. You did it! You got her back!' Janine broke free awkwardly and leaned anxiously into the car to look at Tamsyn again.

'They said that she'd be asleep. When will she wake, do you think? They must have doped her.'

'I've no idea, but let's get her home and if she hasn't woken up by then we'll have the doctor in. Get in. I'll drive. We must go and find Sergeant Harrington.'

'I don't want the police involved any more,' announced Janine, recalling the promise made to her on the telephone.

'We must let him see Tamsyn's really safe,' said Gavin. 'He's in the lorry park, we'll drive across and tell him before we go home. Do get in the car in case Shaw and friends are still about.'

'It's all right,' said Janine, 'the man on the telephone told me if I kept quiet about the whole incident they'd leave us alone. We'll be safe now.' Gavin looked sceptical at this assertion, but unwilling to spoil Janine's moment of joy and new-found hope in the future, he kept his doubts undeclared, contenting himself with a sweeping glance round the car park for signs of danger.

'You must help me persuade Sergeant Harrington to let the whole thing drop now,' went on Janine. 'It's over, Tamsyn's safe and I don't want us living in fear just because the police were determined to try and arrest the drugs ring.'

'We'll talk to him about it at once,' agreed Gavin, still not happy about the rather naïve trust Janine appeared to have in the easy conclusion of the affair. 'Get in the car and we'll go over there now. They'll be watching us now and wondering what's happened.' Gavin pushed her gently towards the car door and Janine slid into the seat beside her daughter, handing the keys to Gavin. She was too exhausted to argue and longed to hold Tamsyn in her arms again.

As Gavin went round to the driver's door a man approached and opened the door of the next car. At once Gavin was on his guard, but the man grinned across at him cheerfully.

'Get it going all right, mate?' he enquired.

Gavin looked at him questioningly. 'I'm sorry?'

'The motor,' said the man. 'Find the problem, did you?'

Gavin got into the car and said through the open window, 'What problem?' He put the key in the ignition.

'Wasn't it you under the bonnet earlier?' queried the man. 'Said you were having problems with the starter motor. No, come to think of it, that guy had a moustache. Your car though, mate of yours, was it? Hope it goes all right, anyway.' He got into his own car.

'Just a minute,' called Gavin now very suspicious. He jumped out of the car again and the man wound down his window.

'Are you sure it was this car?'

'Yeh, quite sure. Was here when I parked mine.' With a wave he backed his car out and drove away.

'Janine!' said Gavin sharply. 'Get Tamsyn out and get well clear.'

'What? What's the matter?'

'Don't argue!' shouted Gavin angrily, 'just get out. Fast!'

Galvanised into action by his tone Janine scrambled out of the car and began pulling the inert form of Tamsyn after her. Gavin was with her immediately and together they dragged Tamsyn clear of the car, then Gavin picked her up in his arms and carried her quickly away from the car, Janine following closely behind. Without any undue signs of haste, they strode across the car park past the service buildings to the lorry park beyond. As they approached, the back doors of a green van advertising itself as Donaldson's Parcel Express, opened to reveal the anxious face of Sergeant Harrington. Quickly all three were bundled inside and the doors closed immediately behind them.

The inside of the van was lit with lamps and furnished very like a caravan with table, chairs and a bunk bed down one side. There was even a small stove with a sink beside it. A camera was mounted at a peep-hole in the side and binoculars commanded a view of the car park outside.

Gavin laid Tamsyn on the bunk and Janine covered her with one of the blankets folded at the foot. Briefly then, Gavin explained the situation to the policeman and Harrington nodded in agreement with his reading of it.

'Sounds like a booby trap. Don't worry, we'll get on to it.'

'What?' demanded Janine, transferring her attention from Tamsyn for a moment to the men's discussion. 'What is going on?'

'Someone was seen tinkering with your car,' replied the sergeant. 'We'd just like to check it over before you drive it again.'

'But they said they'd leave us alone,' wailed Janine.

'Darling, they daren't,' said Gavin gently. 'They can't afford to.'

'We're not certain,' said the sergeant, 'but anyway you're safe here.'

'Suppose they saw us coming across?' said Janine shakily, all her earlier fears returning.

'It's a possibility,' admitted the sergeant. 'But I doubt if any of them waited about to see the bomb go off, if there is indeed a bomb. There'd be too many questions asked of everyone in the place. They'd want to be well clear before the service area was sealed off afterwards. Remember they made you wait for half an hour before you went back to your car.'

'But someone was watching me then.'

'So they said. It gave them a head start to let you think so. Now,' went on the sergeant briskly, 'I must get on to this,' and he turned and began speaking on his radio.

Within minutes Janine's car was cordoned off and all the vehicles nearby were removed. Gavin and Janine sat in the van with the still-sleeping Tamsyn, unable to see what was going on.

'I thought it was all over,' said Janine bitterly. 'I thought we were free at last.'

'It was too easy,' replied Gavin gently. 'We have to keep you safe until everyone listed in that note-book has been picked up.'

'But we haven't got the note-book,'

cried Janine. 'They've got the notebook, and it must be what they wanted or they wouldn't have given Tamsyn back.'

'Don't worry . . . ' began Gavin.

'Don't worry!' Janine rounded on him. 'Everyone keeps telling me not to worry. What do you all think I am? A machine? A robot with no feelings?'

Gavin waited for the outburst to finish and then said evenly, 'Before you collected the package with the notebook in it from Powell, the police had already been there and opened it. They made copies of what was inside.'

Janine stared at him, almost overcome with rage. 'How could they?' she breathed with barely suppressed fury. 'How could they do such a thing when they knew Tamsyn's life might be lost because of it?'

Gavin took her hands in his and said softly, 'Janine, they had to. It was a risk they had to take. Suppose they hadn't and Tamsyn had been lost anyway, they'd never have got the men responsible.' Janine jerked her hands away, her eyes still blazing.

'Why couldn't they have told me? At least they could have told me.'

'Could you have sounded convincing if you'd known it had been done? When they asked if it had been opened?'

'Of course, if Tamsyn's life was at stake. Oh, I don't know, maybe not. What about Anthony Powell? He kept asking me what it was all about. He must have known all the time and been expecting me. Suppose they had got to him, he could have ruined everything.'

'He had to know enough not to alert you. It would have looked very suspicious if he hadn't questioned you. But you were marginally safer if you didn't know the police had copies.'

Still angry Janine lapsed into silence. She had no arguments left and at least she had Tamsyn safe.

The sirens of several police cars wailed as reinforcements arrived with officers from the bomb squad. Unable to see, they listened to the confused noise that penetrated the van and then the door opened again to admit Sergeant Harrington and another man.

'Explosives wired to the ignition, turn the key and — boom! It's going to be a long job, I'm afraid,' he said. 'They may have to do a controlled explosion. It's probably best if we get you home. If you can make yourselves comfortable here, Andrews'll drive you home.'

'I've got my car, too, Sergeant,' said Gavin. 'Any reason why we can't use that?'

'I shouldn't, sir, better to play it safe and keep under cover in the van. You never know . . . They may know by now that their little surprise did not work and it would be a pity if they saw Mrs Sherwood leave in a private car, it might give them some more unpleasant ideas. One of my men'll drive your car home, sir, if you prefer to travel with Mrs Sherwood, and one of my men will be in the van as well. Just a precaution.'

Gavin nodded at the wisdom of this and handed over his keys. Harrington turned to the man with him. 'Get

Madison to ride in here with them, Andrews, and Black can cover from the outside.' Turning back to Janine he went on, 'We'll give you a police escort all the way to Chariswood. You'll be quite safe.'

'Chariswood?'

'It would be better for a day or two,' explained Gavin. 'Just until the police have tied up a few loose ends, it would be better if you didn't go home.' Janine sighed and agreed, her fate no longer in her own hands.

Minutes later they eased out of the lorry park, the police escort keeping a discreet distance from the closed van until it was well away from the service area; then they were clear and speeding down the motorway behind their motor-cycle outrider. The motion of the van was soothing and before long, propped up against some cushions and Gavin, Janine slept the sleep of exhaustion.

That evening when all the tales were told and Tamsyn was safely tucked up in bed, Janine sat by the fire in the drawing-room at Chariswood feeling more at ease than she had for days. The doctor had examined both her and Tamsyn and pronounced nothing wrong with either of them that a few days' complete rest could not cure, though Tamsyn was still dazed from the drugs she had been given and the terror with which she had lived for the last few days. Little snippets of her story emerged and Janine learned of the Land Rover skidding off the road by the bridge and the subsequent trek through the snow until they found another vehicle at an outlying farm. She heard of a tiny room in a red-brick building with only the backs of houses as a view from the grubby window; she heard that Tamsyn had been hungry. Of Shaw she heard nothing, the child did not mention him, and she appeared to have no recollection of leaving the tiny room or of travelling to the service area on the motorway. Janine was careful not to press her, not to probe unmentioned aspects of her ordeal, knowing she would hear it all in time if Tamsyn wanted to talk about them. Perhaps her memories were already clouding, Janine could only hope so. The little girl was safe and that was all that mattered.

Having had an afternoon's sleep and an excellent meal, Janine sat curled in an armchair, gazing into the dancing flames, warm and comfortable at last. Lady Hampton and Sandra had left the drawing-room once the coffee tray had been removed and Janine was happy to be alone with her thoughts. Before long, however, the door opened and Gavin appeared. He had eaten dinner with them, but had been strangely withdrawn and reserved during the meal and when they had left the table he disappeared into the library saying he had work to do and he would have his coffee in there. Now he came in and stood with his back to the fire for a moment, looking down at Janine curled into the armchair. Under his scrutiny

Janine uncoiled her legs and sat straight.

'Tamsyn asleep?' he asked lightly. Janine nodded.

'Good. She seems to have survived her ordeal remarkably well.'

'I hope so,' replied Janine. 'Time will tell, she seems resilient enough but there may be some hidden scars.'

'Janine.' Gavin's voice changed, lowered a little, and Janine looked up at him. 'Janine,' he held out both his hands and Janine placed hers in them. Gently he pulled her to her feet and looked down into her face. It was a look of such tenderness that Janine felt shaky, her legs weak, and she lowered her eyes from his gaze.

'Janine, I must talk to you. I would have done ages ago, but events overtook us and it was neither the time nor the place.' He turned her face to his, lifting her chin with his fingers.

'Tell me about Harry.' The question was so unexpected that Janine stared at him for a moment before she replied.

'There's nothing to tell that you don't already know. I want to forget, as much and as quickly as I can.'

Gavin nodded. 'But can you?'

'I might if people stopped asking me about him,' she returned with spirit.

Gavin was silent for a moment and then said, 'I want to tell you something; no, don't speak until I've finished, for I must say it all.' He paused then as if unsure how to go on; then he said, 'I love you, Janine, that you must know already and . . . ' he laid a finger on her lips as she moved to speak. 'I love you with every part of me, my body and my mind, and I want you to be my wife. I want to love you and care for you for the rest of your life. I want Tamsyn as my daughter, I love her as such already, and I want to be the father of your other children.' He let go of her then and turned away abruptly, crossing the room before he faced her again while she watched him in silence. 'But I only want all that if you can forget the past and leave your fears behind you; if you can love me, and me alone, without thought for Harry and the love you once gave him. I'm a selfish man, my darling,' he grinned ruefully, 'and I can't share you with anyone, not even with a ghost or the fear he left behind. If you can come to me unafraid of the future I will do my utmost to justify your trust in me.' He paused then and looking slightly shamefaced he smiled awkwardly and added, 'I'm sorry, I didn't mean to speechify at you.'

'It's because you're afraid too,' said Janine gently, wondering how she had ever considered him arrogant, and yet in the same thought recognising that his gentleness was for her alone.

'Perhaps,' he admitted. 'Maybe I should have swept you into my arms where you belong and be damned to everything else.'

Lightly she ran to him and putting her arms round his neck, looked up into his shadowed face and with adoration in her eyes said simply, 'Gavin, dearest Gavin, I can't live without you,' and she raised her lips to take his. He crushed her into his arms then, and kissed her until they were both breathless. They looked again into each other's eyes and saw such latent passion there, each in the other, that they clung together in silence for a moment before Gavin kissed her again, more gently this time and said, 'Darling Janine, sweetheart of my life.' Taking her hand in his he carried it to his lips and placed a kiss in its palm and asked, 'Can you forgive me for the way I behaved when we first met?'

Janine, with happiness bubbling inside her, said teasingly, 'That depends on whether you're really sorry and admit that you weren't right about me. I can remember not so long ago when I wasn't, in your own words, your first choice.'

'I know, I know. And everything about you has convinced me I was wrong from that moment on. I've been trying to admit it to you ever since.' He paused and then said softly, 'Love me?'

'Yes.'

'Marry me?'

'Yes.'

And neither of them heard the door as Lady Hampton entered and hastily backed out again to go and tell Sandra that Gavin had met his match at last.

THE END